Dolphin Cove Vets

Helping pets and healing hearts…

Best friends and cutting-edge vets Ellie Stone and Drew Trevelyan have realized their dream of owning the best veterinary practice in Cornwall. The clinic lies at the heart of their tight-knit community, and they couldn't be happier.

Except…

No strangers to heartbreak, they've vowed to put their work before anything else, until two new arrivals test their resolve to remain single…

The Vet's Secret Son
by Annie O'Neil

Ellie is shocked when her past collides with her present and she's forced to work with her ex— and to reveal the secret she's hidden from Lucas for six years…

Healing the Vet's Heart
by Annie Claydon

Recovering from a devastating car accident, romance is the last thing on Drew's mind, until Caro finds a way through to his guarded heart…

Both available now!

Dear Reader,

If you've read any of my books you will know that I am crazy mad for animals. I live on a farm and most days it feels a lot like being at Dr. Dolittle's! We have tortoises and chickens, bees, cows, and dogs (who, as I write, are wrestling under my desk), and I love them all. Thanks to them I have also had the pleasure of befriending our local vets— who are AMAZING. They get up in the middle of the night to help with a difficult calving, spend hours giving a C-section to a young heifer in the middle of a field, stand in the pouring rain to pregnancy test our cows. All without having the benefit of having a "patient" who can describe what hurts and what doesn't.

Writing this duet with Annie Claydon was simply the magical icing on the cake. I just adore her and her fabulous creativity. She's also incredibly kind, lovely and every bit as marvelous as my veterinarian friends.

I hope you enjoy the journey to Dolphin Cove. I know I'd move there in a second if it weren't for my beloved menagerie…

xoxo *Annie O'*

THE VET'S SECRET SON

———

ANNIE O'NEIL

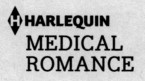

HARLEQUIN
MEDICAL
ROMANCE

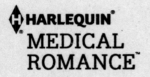

HARLEQUIN®
MEDICAL
ROMANCE™

Recycling programs
for this product may
not exist in your area.

ISBN-13: 978-1-335-14961-9

The Vet's Secret Son

Harlequin Enterprises ULC
22 Adelaide St. West, 40th Floor
Toronto, Ontario M5H 4E3, Canada
www.Harlequin.com

Printed in U.S.A.

Annie O'Neil spent most of her childhood with her leg draped over the family rocking chair and a book in her hand. Novels, baking and writing too much teenage angst poetry ate up most of her youth. Now Annie splits her time between corralling her husband into helping her with their cows, baking, reading, barrel racing (not really!) and spending some very happy hours at her computer writing.

Books by Annie O'Neil

Harlequin Medical Romance

Miracles in the Making
Risking Her Heart on the Single Dad

Pups that Make Miracles
Making Christmas Special Again

Single Dad Docs
Tempted by Her Single Dad Boss

Hope Children's Hospital
The Army Doc's Christmas Angel

Hot Greek Doc
One Night with Dr. Nikolaides

Her Knight Under the Mistletoe
Reunited with Her Parisian Surgeon
The Doctor's Marriage for a Month
A Return, a Reunion, a Wedding

Visit the Author Profile page
at Harlequin.com for more titles.

This one goes out to every veterinarian I have called out of hours and who has come running. I thank you. My beasties thank you. x Annie O'

CHAPTER ONE

ELLIE LIFTED THE small ball of fluff up in front of her face and gave it a nuzzle. Puppy time after a difficult surgery was always curative. 'Who's the best little-bitty puppy?'

The pitch-black Labrador put its paw on her nose then gave her a tiny pink-tongued lick on the cheek. Even though she'd had a million puppy moments like it, Ellie's heart strained at the seams.

'You're definitely the cutest.'

As if in protest, the other puppies—a mad mix of golden, red, black and a solitary chocolate one—began tumbling up and over her legs, vying for cuddles.

Four weeks old and full of life. A perfect litter of ten, spanning every colour of the Labrador spectrum. It was the last litter Esmerelda, Ellie's beloved Lab, would have, and even though she knew she wasn't entirely objective, she was certain it was the best.

She picked up another one and breathed in the sweet, scrummy puppy scent. Mmm... Perfect. She couldn't wait for Mav to get back from surf school. Her son's giggles of delight combined with puppy cuddles...sheer heaven.

'Having a bit of puppy therapy, are we?'

Ellie looked up and saw her long-term mentor smiling down at her. 'Ha! You caught me, Henry.'

'Tough surgery?'

'Very.' She told him about the golden retriever who'd been injured when he'd tripped whilst carrying a big stick.

'And the oropharynx?'

'There was a truckload of splinters in his tongue and his mouth. A huge one was lodged in his throat, the poor lad. He's in Recovery now. I don't know who's feeling worse. Him or his owner.'

Henry gave a sympathetic shrug. 'It's a tough call sometimes. I just had a woman sob the entire time I clipped her cat's nails!'

Ellie made an empathetic noise. 'Mrs Coutts?'

Henry grinned. 'You clearly know your patients' owners well.'

'One of the keys to our success here in Dolphin Cove.' She patted the newspaper-covered play area where she was stretched out, puppies using her like a climbing frame. 'Join me?'

Henry, who'd valiantly stepped in to be her emergency locum vet over the last few months, grinned and sat down opposite her. 'How could I resist?'

The puppies climbed and tumbled over him, vying for cuddles. For someone with a puppy tucked in the crook of each arm, her mentor didn't look all that chirpy.

'You're looking serious. Got a new surgery you need to brainstorm?'

Henry shook his head, his white hair flopping across his forehead as he did so. He looked every bit the mad professor. Semi-retired and as smart as a whip, he was also her hero. Who else in the whole of the UK would've given up their summer holidays to come down to Cornwall and take over the roster of complicated surgeries her business partner had lined up?

She shoved aside the niggle of discomfort the question elicited and smiled at him. Just about no one, that's who. No one she cared to lay eyes on, anyway.

'It's not that,' he said, easing yet another puppy into his arms.

Ah. So there *was* something.

Ellie gently extracted her insanely curly

ponytail from one of the puppy's mouths. One day she'd get her hair under control. She snorted. And one day pigs would fly. 'Not a pull toy, little one,' she cooed, easing a final golden coil out of its gummy mouth.

She inspected Henry as the pup he was holding scampered away and he pulled one of her favourite pups, the only chocolate Lab in the litter, into his lap. He was looking awfully serious.

The chocolate pup put both of its paws on Henry's beard then slid back down into the nook of his arm and instantly fell asleep.

Ellie laughed. 'I guess that was enough playtime for him.'

'Guess so.' Henry cupped the little pup's head in one of his big old hands. His tone was much more reflective than a vet with over forty years of experience might be. He must have seen thousands of puppies curl up into sleepy little balls of fur and puppy snorts over the years.

'C'mon, Henry. Out with it. There's something playing on your mind. You rescued me in my hour of need. If I can do anything to help you in yours, just say the word.'

She wasn't kidding. When Drew, her business partner and her bestie, was in a horrific car accident, Henry came right down. Drew's long stint in hospital was coming to an end, but there was still ample rehab and healing to keep him away from the surgery for at least the next eight to ten weeks. More if there were any setbacks.

Uh-oh. Drew hadn't had a setback had he?

Henry readjusted the puppy and something about the look in his eyes made her scoop one up into her own arms. She gave it a nuzzle as Henry began to speak. When he'd finished, she could hardly hear for the buzzing in her ears.

It wasn't Drew. It was a favour. And not just any old favour. He was asking her to do the one thing she'd promised she would never do. Let Lucas Williams work at Dolphin Cove.

But she owed Henry. She owed him big time.

Four months ago she'd barely held it together when Drew's life hung in the balance. Henry had come to her rescue. Not only did he tackle Drew's incredibly complicated surgeries, he also brought along students from the Royal Veterinary College down for internships to help ease the load. Much to her embarrassment, he used Ellie as an example of what you could achieve if you stuck to your guns: build one of Britain's most innovative veterinary surgeries in one of its most old-fashioned villages even when your heart had just been smashed to absolute smithereens.

Okay.

He didn't say that end bit.

He focussed on the good. Which was how she'd survived her heartache and the epic life change that came in its wake. The Dolphin Cove Veterinary Clinic was literally her dream come true. And now it could all disappear in the blink of an eye. If she let herself be prone to dramatics. Which she was, because…oh, damn!

This felt almost as bad as— No. Nothing felt worse than having the love of her life take back his proposal and throw all of their hopes and dreams to the wayside to become television's favourite celebrity veterinarian.

The Uber-Vet.

Bleurgh.

Uber-Louse more like.

The man on television—which, obviously, she'd only ever watched season after season by total accident—was so far removed from the geeky, funny, hilariously wonderful man she'd fallen in love with she could barely stand to look at him.

So much for *I've got to save my dad's clinic, Ells. I just want to keep everything low-key to*

keep the stress down. I'm all they've got now.
I don't want to ruin your dream.

It scared her to realise how raw the old
wounds still were. Wounds she had done everything in her power to heal as she'd embarked on the new life she'd built for her and
her son.

'He really said you have to go *now*?' Ellie
knew she was repeating exactly what Henry
had just said, but she didn't seem able to get
the facts to sink in.

Lucas Williams, ex-love of her life, wanted
Henry to take over his stupid television show.
Immediately. And to make that happen? He
was going to come to Dolphin Cove and replace Henry.

The skin prickled at the back of her neck.

This was the moment she had hoped
against hope would never happen.

Henry scrubbed a hand through his hair.
He of all people knew what a bit ask it was,
but there was a lot at stake for him as well.
'The students depend on these scholarships,
and with money so hard to come by these
days—'

She waved her hand to get him to stop talking. She, more than anyone, knew how important the scholarships were. There was no
chance she could've attended the Royal Vet-

erinary College without a bursary. Denying other students the chance because of pride? It would be an unspeakably selfish thing to do.

She forced herself to repeat the facts to Henry to make absolutely sure she'd got them right. 'So, what you're saying is, Lucas Williams is giving up his job as the Uber-Vet and he wants you to be the new one?'

'That's right.' Henry nodded. 'We'd film at the veterinary college, raising its profile, and all of the proceeds would go towards scholarships for less well-off students.'

Just like she'd been.

'And you have to go tomorrow?'

'Day after. Lucas is going to drive down tomorrow. The television producers seem to be mad about the idea and they want to start filming...'

'ASAP,' they said in tandem.

She looked out beyond the low wall of the puppy pen to the big old floor-to-ceiling glass windows that faced the private cove beyond the clinic. Still sunny. Still gorgeous. At least something was the same. Another perfect summer's day in Cornwall.

She squinted at the sun. It'd be hours yet before it dipped into the sea, but those hours were quickly evaporating and before she knew it, it would be tomorrow morning, Henry would leave and the man who had changed her life for ever would be arriving. And all of this exactly when she had one of the most important surgeries in Dolphin Cove Veterinary Clinic's entire history on the books.

Prosthetics for a beautiful Bernese mountain dog. A gorgeous beast of a dog called Moose who'd struggled to recover from a car accident a few weeks back. Ellie, a specialist in emergency surgery and internal medicine, had done her best, but had ultimately held up her hands and said, 'It's not enough. This dog needs more.' The type of 'more' only an orthopaedic surgeon could envision. An orthopaedic surgeon exactly like Lucas Williams.

The father of her child. The son he didn't know he had.

She swallowed back an uncomfortable lump of guilt. 'And there's no one else in the entire world who can come down apart from *him*?'

'You want and deserve the best, Ellie. Lucas is the best there is.' She scuffed her foot against the floor exactly the way Maverick would've if she'd told him it was time for bed.

'Of course, I could always turn down the offer and stay here.'

'Don't be ridiculous.' Of course Henry must go. It was a once in a lifetime offer. Putting the finest veterinary college in the UK in the limelight as well as giving its poorer students a critical financial lifeline? There was no way she could insist Henry stay. Even so. 'Just…give me a minute to process this, all right?'

Henry opened his mouth, presumably to say she'd be fine, but…urgh! She didn't want *fine*. She wanted everything to stay exactly as it was. Well. Not *exactly*. She'd rather Drew wasn't in recovery from his accident and that he'd never been through the emotional and physical wringers the past couple of years had thrown at him, but what was the point in working your fingers to the bone and aiming for the moon and the stars beyond it only for life to throw her biggest fear into her path?

A clammy skittering of goosebumps ran across her skin.

She could've done what her parents and Drew had suggested when she'd found out she was pregnant. Told Lucas she was having his son. But to do so precisely when the papers had started crowing about a rumoured engagement between the Uber-Vet and his producer? No chance. Instead, she'd poured all her hurt and anger into building the clinic even Lucas would admire.

She gave her arms a rub as a chill swept through her.

What good was venom or comeuppance when the secret she held would change his life?

Lucas would be angry. He had every right to be. Over five years of not knowing he had a son… She'd be raging if she were in his shoes. But she'd done what she'd done for a reason. Lots of reasons. One of which was ensuring she had full custody of Maverick.

All that might change now.

Who was she kidding? Everything would change once Lucas found out Maverick was his son. Anyone who cared for animals the way he did couldn't be all evil.

Henry slipped the sleeping puppy in his arm onto a bed. 'I'd better get up to the flat and start packing.'

'Don't leave.' Ellie gestured for him to stay then twisted her coils of strawberry blonde curls into a messy topknot. 'Not just yet.'

'How many more weeks until Drew's out of hospital?' Henry asked as he sat back down, even though he knew the answer as well as she did.

'He's home in the next couple of weeks,

but he's got a good two months of rehab before he can come back here to the clinic and even then...' She glowered, the frown quickly softening as a pair of puppies began to climb a small set of steps onto a short slide and...whoosh. So adorable! Maybe she'd give Drew a puppy as part of his rehab. He hadn't seemed so keen on doing all the exercises they'd given him last time she'd visited him in hospital, but once he was home and had a puppy to entice him out on a walk...

'And his recovery is going well?' Henry asked.

What was going on here? Henry had visited Drew practically as much as Ellie had. Saying that... Ellie knew Drew better than just about anyone in the village. Not only was he her best friend from Dolphin Cove, he had been a student alongside Lucas and Ellie at the Royal Veterinary College. He'd watched her fall in love. He'd been part of the plotting and planning for each and every component of their dream clinic. He'd been there to mop up the tears when Lucas had ripped her heart out of her chest and walked away from each and every one of their plans. He'd also been sitting beside her as she'd watched the smiley face appear on that fateful pregnancy test nine weeks after they'd returned to Dolphin

Cove to set up the clinic without Lucas. She'd clocked one missed period up to stress and heartache. Two?

Well.

She had her boy and she loved him to bits, so…not *everything* about her time with Lucas had turned out badly.

She forced herself back onto topic. 'I think it's fair to say being a patient doesn't really suit him.' Poor Drew had already suffered so much loss. If he was permanently disabled because of his leg injuries? Nightmare. She couldn't imagine him living a sedentary life. Not happily anyway. The man was made of motion. Except for these past few months. Suffice it to say her bestie was going to have to pull some hardcore determination out of the bag if he wanted to stand at an operating table for eight-plus hours ever again.

Henry tapped Ellie on the knee, presumably having seen her drift off into A World Without Drew. 'Ellie, love. I know you've been through a lot lately, but I wouldn't be doing this if it wasn't the right thing to do. Think of all of those amazing vets I can send down here for internships.'

Ellie heaved a melodramatic sigh, hoping Henry knew she wasn't actually angry, just… digesting things. 'I know. I should be cracking open the champagne for you. I just… It's one of those crossroads moments.'

'One you, of all people, have the strength to get through.'

'You think?' The last thing she felt right now was strong. Terrified, shaky, anxious and defensive? Definitely. Able to hold her own against the man she'd once loved with every fibre of her being? Not so much.

'You're made of stronger stuff than you ever give yourself credit for,' Henry said, scooching over to her side of the puppy pen and giving her a half-hug. 'Who knows? Maybe it'll be the best thing that ever happened.'

'Ha!' She crinkled her nose up. 'Having the Uber-Vet here is *not* going to be the best thing that ever happened to me.'

'No.' Henry gave his beard a thoughtful stroke. 'But having Lucas Williams here might be.' Henry smiled as if he knew something she didn't then left the room, Ellie's jaw still hanging open in disbelief.

Lucas pulled off the main road, such as it was, and onto the long, wooded drive leading down to the clinic. Seeing the clinic sign and then glimpses of the cove peek through the woodland felt as familiar to him as if he'd done it a thousand times. In a way he had.

They'd talked about every detail of their 'fantasy clinic' a thousand times. More.

Back when this site had been private land, they couldn't have dreamt of affording let alone building a state-of-the-art clinic on it. Dreaming the impossible was easy with Ellie. She was a woman who could look at anything and spot nothing but possibility. Nothing but hope. Which went a long way towards explaining why he'd fallen in love with her the instant she'd walked into that first day of veterinary college wearing a studious expression and a tiger onesie.

It surprised him how raw he felt, seeing their shared dream as a reality he wasn't a part of.

Sure, he was proud of turning his father's failing clinic into something extraordinary, too. It had saved his family from unimaginable problems, but…looking at Ellie's clinic on the website before he'd come down here had stirred something in him he hadn't been sure still existed. *Hope*. Hope that the two of them might be able to find a peace with their complicated past.

Most of the staff photos were action shots, unlike his well-lit posed one taken by the

production photographer. There were loads
of Drew, of course, but the pictures of Ellie
were the ones that had punched him in the
solar plexus. Ellie deep in concentration in
surgery. Ellie playing with the pups she bred
as service dogs from Esmerelda, the puppy
he'd given to her with a diamond ring on her
collar and a question on his lips.

Will you marry me?

If only—

He loosened his white-knuckled grip on
the steering wheel and continued to drive. If
only a lot of things.

As he drove through the woodland, a broad
expanse of lawn opened out before him and
then the drive split—one lane signposted for
the main clinic and community petting zoo
and the other for the surgical ward. He let out
a low whistle.

Ellie and Drew had clearly worked their
socks off. He felt a burst of pride on their behalf and then, in its wake, an all too familiar
stab of guilt.

He steered the car towards the main clinic.
The car park was still relatively full, even
though it was near the end of the day. The
building was a glass, beam and wood-shin-
gled number that oozed confidence and comfort. Exactly the type of place you'd want to

bring your pet if they were hurt. Exactly the type of place he and Ellie had envisioned opening all those years ago. He huffed out a laugh. She'd really gone and done it. With her trusty childhood friend Drew, who she had no doubt fallen in love with by now. Had kids with. Pets of their own.

At least she'd kept Esmerelda.

A dog isn't just for a proposal...

He imagined Drew slipping a ring on Ellie's finger, felt a surge of something fiery and hot fill his chest, then checked himself. He had no rights in that area. And certainly no right to be jealous. Who Ellie loved or didn't love was no longer his business. Helping her was.

He parked the car, clapped his hands together and gave them a rub. He'd waited a long time to make amends. Maybe too long. Tunnel vision had been the only thing that had kept him going as he'd dealt with the massive debt his father's London-based veterinary clinic had accrued as Parkinson's had begun to take its toll on his father's health, then dementia and then, six months ago, his passing.

There were countless other threads to his family's complicated story, and making sure Ellie wasn't mired down with them had made breaking things off seem like the only option. Now, with Henry taking over the reins of the show he'd created to save his family from financial ruin, he felt as if he was breathing freely for the first time in years.

A bell tinkled above his head as he entered the bright, welcoming atrium-style reception area. At its heart stood a small oak tree. The tree, a couple of metres in height, was planted in the centre of a wraparound bench seat where patients and their owners sat waiting for their appointments.

The sight threw him back in time, feeling his hand close over Ellie's smaller, more delicate hand as he'd passed the acorn from his to her palm when they'd decided this was the perfect spot to build their clinic.

From the tiny acorn...

He gave his head a shake. It was probably a fake. Who planted an oak tree in their atrium lobby?

Ellie Stone, that's who.

He scrubbed a hand through his hair and made himself examine the place with a more practised eye. This was, after all, to be his workplace for the next few weeks. If Ellie didn't chuck him out on his ear.

Pushing her reaction to the side, he scanned the atrium. The interior, whilst modern and clearly designed for animals, was as warm and welcoming as a classic country hotel. A huge stone and wood reception desk stood a few metres back from the door. In lieu of the near obligatory plastic chairs or benches most vet surgeries had, the Dolphin Cove Veterinary Clinic had inviting sofas and window seats built into the multi-angled reception area in addition to the bench seat round the tree. There was a floor-to-ceiling cat scratch and even a little cave off in a corner with a sign on it reading 'For pooches who prefer a quiet space.'

Behind the reception desk, a young woman who would've looked more at home on the back of a horse at an elite show jumping event was tapping something into the computer. She looked up when he approached. 'Hello, may I—? Oh, my gawd! Are you...?' She waved at the other two people sitting in the reception area. An elderly woman with a cat in a soft carrying case and a stylish young man with a tiny Pekingese on his lap. 'It's the Uber-Vet!'

Lucas shook his head. Fame and recognition were his least favourite aspects of his job. That and the non-stop rumours about his imaginary engagements. He'd barely had time for dating let alone having enough head space to think about falling in love. And that was the thing, wasn't it? You didn't think about falling in love. You just did it. Precisely as he'd done with Ellie.

'Don't move!' The girl scuttled round the desk with her phone pinched between her immaculately manicured nails, 'Can we do a selfie?'

Check that. Selfies were his least favourite part of being the Uber-Vet.

'I'm getting a selfie with the Uber-Vet!' The girl sing-songed at the two pet owners as Lucas resisted a sigh and put on an obliging smile.

The flash on her phone went off, and then, as she took a couple more, she launched into a monologue. 'I'm Tegan. I work here. Obvs. This is Mrs Cartwright and her very well-loved Siamese cat, Tabatha.' She stage-whispered, 'Bit of a hypochondriac but we love her.' She raised her voice. 'Mrs Cartwright? Would you and Tabatha like your photo taken with the Uber-Vet?'

'Who?' Mrs Cartwright, an immaculately turned-out, birdlike woman, peered at him with bright blue eyes. 'Oh, no,' she said, after she'd given him a quick once over. 'No, thank you. I'll wait for Ellie. As you know, I'd far rather Tabatha saw Drew as he is very familiar with her ailments, but…' She heaved a weary sigh. 'My poor, poor Tabatha.'

Tegan dropped to her knees in front of Tabatha and began making *meow* noises.

'I'd like a photo,' the young man holding the Pekingese said. The dog's immaculately groomed coat flowed over his arms as he swept her up and alongside Lucas. 'Here…' He handed him his phone. 'Can you take it? Your arms are longer. And stronger. My boyfriend would be so totally jel if he knew I was cuddling up to you. Teegs! Come over and get in the photo with us.'

Tegan obliged, happily squishing Lucas into the centre of a Tegan and Pekingese sandwich.

Lucas grinned and bore it. Nearly six years on Britain's television screens had kept his father's clinic from closing and miring his family in debt, so…he held up the phone, 'Ready? Smile!'

When the flash went off, he saw stars for a moment. When they cleared his heart smashed against his chest. There she was.

Ellie Stone. Even more beautiful than he'd remembered her. Wild golden red curls. Her lean, athletic body wearing scrubs as if they'd been handmade for her every curve. A pair of trendy trainers on her feet. No surprise there. Shoes had always been her weakness. Green eyes, as pure and welcoming as the sea beyond the clinic. They flashed brightly then narrowed.

Maybe not so welcoming.

'You're late.'

'Ellie!' Tegan swotted at her arm. 'Don't be rude. It's the Uber-Vet!'

'I know exactly who he is,' she bit out.

'Cool.' Tegan grinned. 'Then you won't mind if I run out and get Torky, yeah?' She turned to Lucas and gave his arm a squeeze. 'He's my twin and, like, totally wants to be a vet, just like you.'

Lucas sucked in a breath. Not the right thing to say in front of your boss who was an excellent vet herself.

Tegan continued, oblivious to the icy stare Ellie was giving her. 'Ells? Would you take our picture when we get back? Me and Torks. What? Why are you so frowny?'

Lucas's eyes zapped to Ellie's. He'd stupidly held onto a sliver of hope that enough time had passed that she might be the tiniest bit happy to see him. She arched an eyebrow as if to say, *This is a veterinary clinic, not a red carpet.*

No smile. No glimmer of delight. No, *Oh,*

my goodness, my Prince Charming has just walked through the door.

Not quite the happy reunion he'd been hoping for.

Ellie sniffed and gave Tegan what he used to teasingly call her 'Mum look'. Teasing because he'd imagined her giving that look to their own children one day. He'd loved that look. Hell. Who was he kidding? He'd loved all her looks. Happy, triumphant, giddy, loving…

'I do mind, Tegan. Torquil is busy in the surgical ward and you should be busy answering the phone.' She tipped her head towards the reception desk, where the phone was, indeed, ringing.

Tegan, full of attitude, swept back behind the reception desk and very pointedly answered the phone, 'Hello, Dolphin Cove Veterinary Clinic, Tegan speaking. How may I help you?'

'Sorry about that—' Lucas began, but Ellie cut him off with an eye-roll.

'She's young. She'll get over it.'

'It's good to see you, Ellie,' Lucas said, meaning it. 'How are you?'

She crossed her arms over the dark blue scrubs dotted with…were those toy poodles?…

and glowered at him. Funny how toy poodles took the edge off a glare.

'Hmm. Good question.' She tapped her chin with her index finger. 'Do you mean… how *are you*, Ellie, after six years of not ever speaking to you? Or, how are you, Ellie, seeing me swan into your clinic as if I owned the place. Or…wait a minute.' She put her finger up in the air as if a lightbulb had just gone off, her green eyes blazing with emotion. 'Best yet…how *are you*, Ellie, after I dumped you and made it very clear there was no place in my life for you despite the fact *you* were the one to always say there is no I in team?'

'*What?*' screeched Tegan from the reception desk, hand over the phone receiver. 'You used to date the Uber-Vet? Ells. You are a dark horse, girlfriend! Ellie and the Uber-Vet. Who knew?'

'His name's Lucas!' Ellie ground out.

At the same time Lucas said, 'Lucas is just fine.'

'Ah! Lucas!' Henry appeared from one of the long corridors stretching out beyond the reception desk. 'There you are. I see you've caught up with Ellie.'

'Henry.' Ellie wheeled on him. 'This was a terrible idea. I'm going to find someone else.'

'Someone else to who can do the Bernese

surgery?' Lucas said, knowing he was on solid ground. 'I don't think so. The only one on the British Isles who can do that surgery is standing right here.'

Ellie opened her mouth, presumably to protest, but nothing came out.

'Oh, dear. Well, I...' Henry's eyes bounced between the pair of them as his brows dived towards his nose in consternation.

'Actually, Henry,' Lucas continued with a smile, 'Ellie and I were just discussing where I should put my things. Weren't we, Ellie?'

'We were doing no such thing,' she growled.

'Oh, well.' Henry gave his beard a thoughtful stroke. 'You're more than welcome to stay in the guest flat with me. I believe there's a sofa bed for the night or I can move out of the bedroom tonight and sleep on the—'

'No!' Ellie snapped. 'My house? My rules. My veterinary clinic? My decision whether or not you even touch one solitary hair on an animal's head.'

The young man with the Pekingese piped up, 'It's a bit late for that. He's already held my Audrey here.'

Ellie's eyebrows shot up to her hairline. 'And you are?'

'Caspian Smythe-Bingham.'

She opened her mouth, presumably to say

'Who?' when a look of recognition flared then softened her features into a welcoming glow of recognition. 'Caspian, yes, of course. I'm ever so sorry. I'm not normally so…um…' She gave Lucas a dismissive flick of her eyes then looked at Henry. 'Henry, if you don't mind showing our *temporary* guest into the coffee room, I'll meet with you both after we take a look at… Audrey, right?' She reached out her hands for the Pekingese who curled up against his owner's chest.

'Oh, no.' Caspian stroked his dog's long hair. 'Audrey doesn't seem to like you.'

Ellie gave a nervous laugh. 'Not to worry. Sometimes it takes a minute or two to get to know one another. Why don't you bring her into the examination room, and we'll take a look there?'

Caspian arched an imperious eyebrow. 'If you don't mind, I'd really rather the Uber-Vet took a look at her. They have a bond already, you see?'

The expression on Ellie's face was so cross it took all of Lucas's power not to laugh. Not that he wanted to irritate her more than he had, but…this was actually a little bit funny. Maybe the funnier later variety of funny, but…

'Why are you laughing?' Ellie's glare bored into him.

'I'm not laughing.'

'Course you are,' Ellie snipped. Her eyes darted to the door as a young boy and an older woman who looked very familiar came in. Ellie's entire demeanour changed. 'Exam room three,' she crisply instructed Lucas. 'You take Audrey. We'll all have a look.'

'Only if you're sure.' Stepping on her toes was the last thing he wanted to do.

'Of course I'm sure.' She pointed him down the corridor towards the exam room then gave a little hip-height wave to the two who'd just come in.

'Did you want to see them?'

'No,' she snapped. When her eyes met his, the sparks flew hard and fast. Like a fresh log had been thrown on a bed of hot coals that had been lying in wait…smouldering…waiting for the perfect moment to flare and burn as brightly as they once had.

'Right you are, then.' Lucas stepped to the side so that Caspian could follow Ellie. 'After you.'

With a rather pointed swish, Ellie whirled around and headed down the corridor as briskly as her trademark trendy trainers would take her. Henry mouthed a silent *'Good luck'* to Lucas as he followed in her wake.

It was going to be an interesting few weeks.

Truth be told, he hadn't been convinced she'd let him in. But now that she had he was going to keep his foot firmly in the door, no matter how many times she tried to slam it. The fire in her eyes had told him everything he'd needed to know. There was something to salvage between them. And he wasn't leaving until he found out exactly what it was.

CHAPTER TWO

ELLIE DIDN'T THINK her heart had ever hammered so hard.

She pictured the village defibrillator in the old-fashioned phone box outside her parents' pub just in case her heart decided to fly straight out of her chest and directly into Lucas's very lovely surgeon's hands.

Err…no! Her heart would stay precisely where it was, thank you very much.

Then why was her hand shaking as she reached out to close the exam-room door?

She'd known Lucas was coming. For an entire twenty-four hours.

Time in which she'd steeled herself to see him. Made plans even.

She had decided to be cool, calm, collected, introduce him to his son, make it clear he'd never ever have custody and then send him on his merry way.

So what had she done instead?

Not prepped her son at all. Made a panicked phone call to her parents then hung up before she could take any of their advice, paced and paced and paced in between trying to sleep, which had worked for about… oh, sixty seconds.

Only to go berserk and all but bare her soul in front of the entire village.

Well.

A bit of her soul in front of two villagers and one visitor who wanted his pet to be seen by Lucas and not her. Still. Talk about heaping one humiliation on another.

As the exam-room door clicked shut, she turned round, only to find herself face to chest with the chest she had once been so familiar with that it was pure instinct to reach out and touch it. As she stood, hand raised between them, Lucas asked, 'Where do you want me?'

Their eyes caught and locked. Electricity buzzed between them, just as it had the night of their very first kiss all those years ago. His clear blue eyes bored into her, asking about a hundred questions all at once.

Am I forgiven? Do you mind that I'm not leaving even if I'm not? What have you been up to for the past six years?

Uh…having and raising the son I still have to tell you about.

'I'll just put Audrey here, shall I?' Caspian's plaintive tone mercifully pulled Lucas's attention away from her. Her nerve endings crackled with discomfort as he settled in front of the exam table as naturally as if he'd worked in this room for years. He'd always had that knack. Putting people instantly at ease. The Lucas Effect, she'd called it. No one was immune. Even a young Cornish girl who'd never been to London or had sushi or a million other things life in Dolphin Cove hadn't prepared her for.

One glimpse of that warm smile of his and…swoon!

And look at him now. Taking over her patients as easily as he'd stepped in front of the cameras and won Britain's heart over as the Uber-Vet.

Uber-Jerk, more like.

She gave him a sidelong glance as she washed her hands and popped on a pair of gloves. Where was the goofy, nerdy funster she'd fallen in love with?

The glasses had been replaced by contacts. Laser surgery?

The short haircut complete with cowlick was gone.

Even the usual glob of jam or spaghetti on his shirt was nowhere to be seen. Just an immaculately kitted out 'smart casual' ensemble, which he filled to perfection.

Nope. The twenty-something veterinary science geek was gone and in his place was the suave, sophisticated and properly grown-up Uber-Vet.

Lucas gave the Pekingese a scratch on the head and an admiring look. Owners loved that and Caspian was no exception.

If Caspian looked at him any more adoringly, sugar cubes would start popping out of his eyes.

In fairness, it was difficult not to be sucked into the Lucas Williams vortex of lust. His dark blond hair was combed back in a wavy invitation to run your fingers through it. His sea-blue eyes spoke volumes, darkening when he saw an injured or abused animal, flashing with a jewel-bright brilliance when he did things like, oh, propose to a woman with a puppy only to take it back the next day. A few freckles. A crooked front tooth that made his dazzling smile just a tiny bit mortal.

Water under the bridge, love. You've put it off long enough. Find a way to have him in your life for Maverick. Your boy deserves to know the truth. So does Lucas.

Ellie could hear her mother's earlier counsel as clearly as if she was in the room. Even so, she hoped her mother had seen that Lucas had arrived and had steered Mav straight to the 'puppy wing', as her son had taken to calling the purpose-built whelping and puppy-rearing pens at the far end of the clinic when she'd dropped him off. He loved it there. Seeing the puppies born and raised before being given to the various families who fostered them until they were old enough for training at specialised centres around the country.

As they all shifted into place around the exam table, a waft of Lucas's man scent enveloped her. How a Londoner managed to smell of warm summer air, freshly chopped wood and oranges was beyond her. She began to mouth-breathe, asking herself on a loop why she hadn't given him his marching papers the instant she'd laid eyes on him.

She'd known this moment was coming ever since she'd seen that smiley face on the pregnancy test. You'd have thought six years would've given her enough time to prepare herself and her son, but…nope! No such luck.

'Ellie?'

'Hmm?'

Lucas gave her a look. The kind that meant

she'd been staring at him but not actually speaking words.

'Mind if I get started?'

'Not at all.' Why would she? Just because the father of her child had re-entered her life seemingly out of nowhere was absolutely no reason to get all tetchy about when he started a canine exam.

Smile and nod.

She should call Drew. Drew would know what to do. He'd been the one to tape her together all of those years ago when her life had fallen apart and come back together in a totally different shape. Drew, who was still in hospital healing from all sorts of injuries—emotional and physical—himself. No. She should not call Drew. She was a grown woman perfectly capable of handling herself in this entirely unnatural situation.

Work!

That was something she knew how to do.

She grabbed her tablet and began tapping in Audrey's details. She pulled up her chart from a previous visit and placed it on the exam table so Lucas could see it.

'About three years, is she?' Lucas asked.

Caspian all but swooned. 'Oh, my goodness, me. *Yes!* How did you know? Are you, like, an animal whisperer as well?'

'Erm, no… Ellie's just pulled up her chart.'

'Oh, right, well, I'm sure it doesn't have all of the details because we've only been here once before, when poor little Aud had a sliver. We live in London, where you are based if I'm not mistaken?' Caspian didn't pause for breath, launching into a long story about how he was down for the weekend, visiting his Aunt Viola.

Ellie tuned in. Her hunch in the reception area had been right. Caspian was one of Viola Smythe-Bingham's great-nephews. Viola had five cats, a pair of wolfhounds, a herd of alpacas and a nineteen-year-old pony called Arthur, all of which were under Ellie's care.

Caspian must be down on one of his annual 'make sure I'm listed in the will trips' Viola frequently complained about. Viola was very rich, very single and had no children of her own. And her family never let her forget it. What they didn't know was that Viola had made an incredibly generous donation towards the construction of their new clinic after they had saved her favourite alpaca, Starburst, from certain death. She had also promised a substantial donation to the Dolphin Cove Veterinary Clinic when she passed away. At ninety-two Viola showed few signs of slowing down. Ellie hoped she never died. Viola was far more fun than any stack of money would be. So were her alpacas.

As Caspian wittered on about Audrey's pedigree, her agility classes, her specialised diet and grooming routine, Ellie's gaze drifted back to Lucas, who was nodding along whilst deftly examining the dog who, although looking a bit wan and listless, was also gazing up at him as if he were a Greek god.

Traitors. The lot of them.

She wondered when Drew came back if he would go all googly-eyed, too. Ask his advice on everything. Treat him like the superstar he was and always would be.

Audrey yelped when Lucas palpated her tummy, then tried to climb into his arms. For comforting, no doubt. Arms that had failed to comfort her when he'd explained he wasn't breaking up with her because he didn't love her but because he didn't want to 'drag her down'. Drag her into the limelight more like. She wasn't nearly as camera ready as the women she saw on his arm at all those star-studded charity events he attended. The swine. He made it very, very difficult to hate him seeing as he had single-handedly quadrupled the amount of donations Britons gave to animal charities.

Wasn't life just great?

Her heart softened as she pictured her gorgeous boy. She wouldn't have him without Lucas. So for that alone she owed him a thank you.

'Her gums are a bit pale and her tummy does seem sore. Ellie, sorry, where do you keep your stethoscopes?'

'My what?'

Caspian and Lucas were both looking at her expectantly.

'Stethoscope?' Lucas took one of his lovely, beautiful surgeon's hands—hands she'd traced again and again with her own fingertips—and put it to his broad expanse of chest as if explaining it to a five-year-old.

She did a weird *ha-ha-ha* laugh. 'I know what a stethoscope is.'

'I know,' He gave her a funny look and put his hand on the small of her back just as he used to whenever her nerves had got the better of her.

She lurched backwards, then gave him a wide-eyed look, pretending his touch hadn't just swept through her body in a honeyed spray of heated sparkles. 'I would've thought the Uber-Vet would have his own, super-special stethoscope.'

Everything at the Uber-Vet's was 'super special'.

Not that she'd watched the show.

Much.

The comment hung in the air like a discordant note.

It had been a low blow. And not really her style. She wasn't a sniper.

'As you know, I'm not the Uber-Vet any more.'

Caspian gasped and asked for details. Ellie pulled out the stethoscope she always kept stuffed in her front scrubs pocket and handed it to him with what she hoped was an apologetic look.

Lucas popped the ear tips in and pressed the chest piece to Audrey's tiny frame.

Caspian lowered his head in a reverent silence as Lucas's features shifted into a deeply attractive expression of studied concentration.

No, she chided herself. It was not attractive. And he probably wasn't even listening.

The Lucas Williams she'd once believed he was didn't exist. That Lucas Williams had been the kindest, most generous, gentle, intelligent, capable, loving man she had ever had the privilege to meet.

This one?

This one was a stranger to her.

We'll start our own practice, we'll get married, we'll have a family of our own.

Urgh. Why did it still hurt so much?

Because all of his reasons had felt like lies in the end.

It had been a Grand Canyon-sized break-up and just like the river that ran through it, she could already feel the self-loathing, disbelief and hurt wash back into her system.

The air in the exam room suddenly felt stifling. She had to get out.

'May I...?' She scooched round the examination table, trying not to brush up against him. All six feet two of his gorgeously fit body. The body she'd once thought would be the one that, at the end of a long day at the clinic, would curl round her in bed, tugging her into his perfect arms. Kiss her with his perfect lips.

Tingles began blossoming in a most inconvenient area at the memory of their kisses.

Anyway.

Lucas looked up, unhooking the stethoscope from his ears. 'You're not leaving, are you?'

Ha-ha-ha. 'No. I was just...erm...finding the scale.' She slipped a small scale onto the exam table and lowered her voice an octave, trying to sound soft and demure and, more to the point, like the owner of the veterinarian surgery they were standing in as she addressed Caspian. 'So, Audrey here has been under the weather?'

Caspian gave her a quick glance then poured all his attention on Lucas, explaining how Audrey had gone off her food and he was ever so worried.

As he rattled through Audrey's diet, Ellie noticed the dog constantly trying to nuzzle into Caspian. More specifically, into Caspian's pocket.

'What have you got in there? Cheese?'

Caspian went deadly serious. 'No. It's her treat food.'

'Which is…?'

'*Foie gras*. It's not normally *foie gras*, but Audrey does hate car travel so I fed her a bowlful last night and then again this morning…but since we've arrived…' He threw up his hands in despair. 'She's been vomiting and exhausted and plodding around as if the weight of the world is around her neck. I've tried and tried to give her more to cheer her up. She likes the scent but won't eat it!'

Ellie tried to keep the judgement out of her voice when she said, 'Perhaps that's because *foie gras* is effectively poisonous to dogs.' Grapes, onions, garlic and almost pure fat? A classic recipe for a good old-fashioned case of pancreatitis.

Lucas took a step back from the exam table. He knew the rule and, astonishingly, was adhering to it. One vet gave the news, the other vet nodded along unless vet number one was floundering and even then...you had to wait for the signal. Theirs had been a tug on an earlobe.

The blood had drained from Caspian's face. 'You mean I've poisoned my precious Audrey?' He clutched the dog to him, her mournful eyes meeting his as if to say, yes, you have.

Lucas and Ellie flew into action. If it was indeed pancreatitis and poor Audrey's distended belly meant a severe, potentially lethal infection was underway, they needed to act and fast.

Ellie swiftly put a drip into her little leg after Lucas had shaved a small spot, despite Caspian's cries of despair. 'It's critical that if she's lost any fluids they be replaced.'

They spent the next few minutes with Ellie doing a more studied examination of Audrey and, after escorting Caspian to the kennel area of the clinic and assuring him he could visit Audrey as often as he liked, they finally convinced him that what she really needed was a good rest and monitoring by their team of vet nurses.

'And you'll call me if anything goes...you know...' Caspian's voice caught in his throat, unable to voice his worst fear. She got it. She felt the same way about her pets.

'I promise we'll ring. Well done for noticing she needed care.' She gave his shoulder a squeeze then added, 'Do give my best to your Aunt Viola, won't you?'

'Course, darling.' Caspian leant in for a kiss on first one cheek and then the other. 'And sorry about, you know, earlier.'

She smirked a 'yeah right' after he'd left, only to have her expression freeze when she saw her son running towards the front door. 'Maverick?' Her heart leapt into her throat as she rushed out to meet him. 'What are you doing there?'

He held out a notebook and pen in his hands. 'I wanted to get the Uber-Vet's autograph. Torky told me he was in here. Can I, Mum?'

His little forehead, high like his father's, was crinkled all the way up his brow. She swept a hand through his dark blond hair, his bright blue eyes looking up at her with such hope. Such expectation.

How could she say no to that face? How could she explain that what he was asking was so much more complicated than asking

for a celebrity's autograph? Lucas Williams
wasn't just the man who'd broken her heart.
He was also Maverick's father. The fear that
had haunted her ever since she discovered
that she was carrying this little boy swept
through her afresh. The fear that Lucas would
take him away from her.

'Ah! There you are, Ellie. I thought maybe we
should sit down and—' Lucas stopped. Ellie
was kneeling in front of a little boy who was
holding a notebook and pen. His little forehead was screwed up as if he was trying to
digest some very complicated information.
When he saw Lucas, his eyes brightened and
his big ear-to-ear smile instantly made Lucas
smile, too.

'Mum, look! It's him! He's still here!'
Ellie stood up so fast she wobbled.
Lucas reached out a hand to steady her,
but she pulled back as if his touch burnt her.
'I'm Maverick.' The little boy stepped forward, his hands holding out his notebook. 'I
wanted to get your autograph, but my mum
said you'd gone back to London.'
'Lucas is very busy, love. He's got a patient.' She nodded towards the elderly woman
sitting patiently with her cat.
Lucas threw Ellie a confused look and

caught a flare of guilt lance through her green eyes. She looked pale, her hands shaking as she feebly tried to wave away her white lie. He looked back at the little boy, registered his hair colour, his eye colour, the way they sloped a bit, like his mother's…and his. Almond shaped, he called them. Sleepy sexy, Ellie had called them. He had the strangest feeling of déjà vu. As if he was looking at a photo of himself from when he had been a little boy.

He tried to estimate the little boy's age and then, with the power of a lightning strike, he got it.

Maverick was his son.

His heart crashed against his ribcage with a ferocity he wouldn't have believed possible.

One look at Ellie, eyes bright with a sheen of tears, and he knew he was right.

Trying his best not to frighten the boy, who quite clearly did not know Lucas was his father, he knelt down in front of him, took the paper and signed it, drawing in his signature pawprint at the end of the 's' in Williams.

This was not the way he'd expected to meet his son. Not even close.

He felt Ellie's eye boring into him throughout the short interlude.

When he looked up at her, she was shaking her head, *No, no, no—don't you dare tell him.*

So what was he meant to do? Leave?

Not a chance.

Emotions assaulted him like knife wounds. Elation. Pride. Loss at having missed so many precious moments. His birth. His first word. His first tooth. Disbelief that Ellie had kept Maverick a secret all these years.

He knew things hadn't ended with any sort of grace between them but hiding a *child*? *His* child? What the hell had she been thinking? This little boy...this gorgeous little boy was his flesh and blood. More than any of their shared hopes and dreams, Ellie knew he'd wanted a family of his own. With her! But life had ripped that possibility away from him.

And now, thanks to her, he'd missed the first five years of his son's life.

He forced his raging thoughts into a cage as he reminded himself, thanks to Ellie, he had a son. A beautiful, healthy, happy little boy. But at this moment? The gratitude ended there. She should have told him.

He rose and looked her straight in the eye. 'You and I need to talk.'

Fifteen minutes later, after a delighted Maverick had been assured he would be able to introduce Lucas to the puppies he and

Torky were currently playing with and Mrs Cartwright was assured, once again, that her beautiful Siamese, Tabatha, was in fine fettle, Ellie shakily handed Lucas a mug of hot tea in the small kitchen that stood at the heart of the immaculate surgical ward.

'Two sugars with milk,' she said before he could ask and then, 'So…'

'Yeah.' He scrubbed a hand through his hair, noticing Ellie's pupils were dilated and her eyes had gone that green-grey colour they'd used to turn when her emotions had been running riot. 'So…'

'Mav's…' she began, her voice catching in her throat. 'Maverick's yours. In case you were wondering.'

'Oh, I figured that out.' Maverick, now that he'd spent a few more minutes with him, was a little carbon copy of him. 'I just— Ells—'

'Don't call me that,' she interrupted. Her eyes were darting everywhere but at him.

'What? Do you want me to call you Miss Stone?' He glanced at her hands. 'Or is it Mrs now?'

'No,' she snapped. 'I'm a single mum.'

A complex fury that she'd gone through this all of this on her own swept through him. 'You didn't have to be.'

She rolled her eyes at him. 'Oh, really? Because I thought when you told me the engagement was off, that meant you didn't want to marry me.'

She opened her mouth to continue then clamped it shut. There was clearly a lot more on her mind, but she wasn't going to make this easy on him. In some ways? Deservedly so. But keeping the fact he had a son from him? It was an unforgivable omission.

'So… I'm guessing you decided not to tell me because of the split?' Not the best of conversation starters, but…he wasn't going to let her clam up.

Her eyes widened. 'Seriously? Lucas, there were a thousand reasons why I didn't tell you.'

His anger was simmering so close to the surface he forced himself to take a drink of the sweet tea rather than lash out and make it incredibly clear that nothing in the world was more important than family. And this little boy… Maverick…was his son.

The few seconds of silence afforded him a vital reminder that he'd been in a desperate place and, he supposed, she must've been, too. Even so… He levelled his voice. 'How about giving me one of them?'

She scrunched her eyes tight and pressed her thumbs to the bridge of her nose. When she opened her eyes again, instead of seeing the guilt and fear he'd seen before he saw strength. The fierce love of a mother determined to protect her son. 'I didn't think you were in a place to handle a son as well as your other "more relevant" responsibilities.'

He flinched at the turn of phrase. His own. Back then he'd been less experienced at juggling his family problems with his romantic life. He'd grown up a lot since then and had definitely learned to choose his words more carefully, but this…this was whiplashing him straight back to a time and place he'd hoped to never revisit.

'It was a complicated time.'

'Complicated?' Ellie's laugh was utterly bereft of humour. 'It seemed pretty straightforward to me. You dumped me to "help your family", then swanned off to become a media darling without me.'

'That wasn't how it happened, Ellie.' He'd been crushed between a rock and damn tight hard place. His options had been limited and by limited he meant he'd had one choice.

Ellie put on a posh voice. 'Swanning into the limelight and dazzling the UK's female fans with your many talents.' Her tone turned dark. 'No wonder you sent me back to my poky village to get on with "a country girl's hopes and dreams".' She crossed her arms de-

fensively. 'You told me I'd be better off without you. Admit it, Lucas. It wasn't that you
didn't want to drag me down. It was that you
wanted to push your own star higher.'

The tang of bile rose in his throat.

His father had been barely able to work because his Parkinson's had become so bad. His
mother had been exhausted from worry and
being his full-time carer. His older brother,
also a vet, had up and vanished. A string of
debts Lucas had uncovered had explained the
disappearance. So he'd been the only one left
to try and keep the debt-ridden clinic afloat.
There was no way he had wanted to subject
Ellie to that. Crush her dreams. Sideline her
while his focus had to be on his family.

The show had come about through a completely chance encounter. One day, a couple of
weeks into his gruelling schedule, a woman
had come in with a dog she'd found that had
been hit by a car. She'd stayed throughout the
exam and had insisted he talk her through
the operation when they'd discovered he had
a broken pelvis. Lucas had organised for her
to watch him operate on the poor little chap
on a monitor they had in one of the private
waiting rooms.

When he'd come out of the operating theatre, she'd told him she was a TV producer

and that watching him at work had given her an idea. The Uber-Vet. The money they had offered him had gone a long way to keeping the clinic open, getting his father proper medical care and his mother some much-needed rest. So Lucas had lunged at the offer and done what he could to make the show a success. A slick haircut and slightly whiter teeth hadn't changed who he was inside!

He'd wanted to tell Ellie when the offer had come in, but the producers had been very clear. They'd wanted him and only him. The idea of ringing her with yet another rejection had simply been out of the question. So he'd signed on the dotted line and got to work.

He gave his jaw a scrub. Yeah. He'd made mistakes. But his choices about how to save his family from crippling debt weren't up for discussion now. Why she had kept his son a secret was. 'Pushing you away was not what I wanted. You know that, Ellie. I needed to help my family and, as I said, things were complicated.'

Ellie's green eyes met his in a blaze of indignation. 'You're right. What would a simple country girl like me know about all those big complicated city things?'

'Ellie—stop it. Don't put yourself down.'

'It's hard not to, sitting face to face with

the one person who I stupidly thought would always put me first.'

Her words landed in his gut like a boulder. Rock. Hard place.

He was feeling the squeeze all over again. Only this time…this time the only person he had to look out for was himself. Complications with his father's Parkinson's had taken his life a couple of years back. He'd built up enough of a rainy-day fund to keep his mother busy with her charity lunches, and as for Jonty? He'd finally resurfaced. Was getting the help he needed for a gambling problem he'd hidden from them for far too long.

Ellie clapped her hands to her face, took in a couple of slow breaths then dropped them to the table with a slapping sound. They had to sting but maybe, like him, her body was buzzing with the type of adrenaline no one should experience. Fear of loss.

She wove her fingers together then finally met his gaze. 'I was going to call you when I found out I was pregnant.'

'When was that?' He was hungry for details.

'About nine weeks after you chose fame and fortune over a humble life in the country.' She took a pointed sip of her tea, her eyes glued to his. 'And a new girlfriend.'

Lucas felt as though a searing hot knife had been slipped between his ribs. 'What? I didn't have a new girlfriend!'

'Katrina Shandwick would probably beg to differ,' Ellie parried, then pushed herself up and away from the wooden table and began muttering something he couldn't make out apart from the 'Don't let him see you cry' part.

Katrina Shandwick had been his producer. They'd gone to countless red-carpet events and she'd always insisted she be his plus one, but it had never been anything more than that—mostly because he'd had no idea how to talk to the press. Especially in the beginning.

As Ellie noisily washed her mug at the sink, every part of him ached to go to her, hold her in his arms, but instinct told him to stay away. Especially if he wanted to be involved in his son's life.

'Ells—Ellie,' he corrected himself. 'Did you really think I would've started dating someone so soon after we split? I'm not like that. And I would never suggest that you or your work were anything less than exemplary. C'mon. That's not me. You knew me better than anyone.'

'Precisely.' Ellie whirled around. 'I *used* to know you. This guy here?' She circled her hand in the air between them. 'I have no clue who he is. You changed overnight. And there was no way I was going to let you into my son's life.'

Our son, he said silently, and then, because he knew he had to fix this if he wanted any sort of relationship with Maverick, 'Ellie, there have been some seriously crossed wires here. I don't think you understand what—'

Ellie cut him off quick smart. 'You're right! I don't understand a thing! I don't understand how, after six years of blanking me, you could just swan in—'

'I hardly swanned in.'

'Selfies in the exam room? Stealing my patients?' She arched an imperious eyebrow. 'Taking forever to diagnose Audrey?' A shadow flickered across her features as an idea struck. 'Oh, my God. You waited, didn't you? You *let me* figure out what was wrong with her to cut me a break? In front of my *own* patient? Are you trying to do me favours? What the actual freaking heck, Lucas? I don't need favours. Especially not from you.'

Lucas looked over his shoulder as if an invisible crowd was giving Ellie hints—the role of the producers in his previous life. If three days ago could count as previous. 'I did no such thing,' he protested, nanoseconds too late. He had. It was her clinic. Her diagnosis to make. He'd done enough guest visits to know it rankled other vets that pet owners would hang on his every word rather than their loyal, committed, local vet. One of many downsides of being part of the fame game.

Ellie dropped her head into her hands again, groaning with the injustice of it all.

'Can't you just go? Go and pretend none of this ever happened?'

'Now that I know I have a son?' He wasn't going to broach the other part—the part about how his heart had stood still when he'd first laid eyes on her. 'Not a chance.'

'Fine,' she eventually said. 'But you're not staying here.'

'But Henry said you needed help—'

Ellie cut him off. 'Thanks to your offer to Henry, I have no choice but to accept your help in the clinic. But, believe me, if we didn't have so many important surgeries coming up, you'd be in your car heading back to the bright lights of London right now.' She huffed out a sigh. 'What I meant was you're not staying *here* here.' She flashed him a look that spoke volumes. She still had feelings for him. Hurt ones definitely. But pain was a bedfellow of love and…damn, this was complicated. Did he still love her?

'Not until I work out how we're going to tell my son you're his…' She gave a little shudder, unable to actually say the words. She pointed up to the ceiling. 'Mav and I live upstairs in a two-bedroomed flat, all the beds are taken. Henry's in the guest flat next door. Ditto. You'll stay…' A slow satisfied smile crept onto her lips. A smile that unleashed another hammering of heartbeats against his bruised ribcage. 'You'll stay at the Hungry Pelican.'

'What? With your parents?'

Ellie's expression went all doe-eyed. 'You're not frightened of seeing my parents, are you? After breaking their little girl's heart, leaving her to raise your son on her own and crushing all her hopes and dreams about love?'

A flicker of something he couldn't quite identify darkened her eyes, though her smile remained bright. Guilt maybe? Had her parents encouraged her to tell him? If they had… excellent. Far be it from him to disagree.

'Great.' He clapped his hands together and gave them a rub. 'If I remember correctly, they're about a two-minute drive away?'

'Or a ten-minute walk,' she answered, and

then, a bit superciliously, 'The Dolphin Cove residents are trying to keep city slickers and their big fancy cars out of the town centre. You know, preserve that country feeling.'

Lucas covered his mouth to mask a smile. Here was the Ellie he knew. The mischievous one who drew the best out of people whether they liked it or not. 'Great. Say the word and I'm ready to go.'

CHAPTER THREE

Ellie flung the pub door open and stomped inside.

'Hello, darling!' her mother trilled from her usual post in the kitchen pass, where she slid gorgeously delicious plates of food through to the serving staff. 'I wasn't expecting you tonight.'

'I've brought you a guest,' Ellie said tightly. 'A *paying* guest.'

'Actually,' Lucas firmly corrected in a low voice, 'I think you'll find I'm family.' He raised his voice again. 'But I'm more than happy to pay.' A steely determination added a timbre to his voice Ellie hadn't remembered hearing before and that six-year-old thread of guilt cinched just the tiniest bit tighter round her heart. Tighter still when her mother appeared in front of them.

Lucas stepped out from behind her and towards her mum. 'Hello, Mrs Stone. It's been a long time…'

Her mum held up a hand, her expression impossible to read. 'Stop right there.' Wyn disappeared from sight and reappeared moments later with Ellie's father Gordon—Gordo to friends. He normally looked like a cross between Santa Claus and your typical jolly old sailor type. Right now, he looked like a very protective father.

'Lucas,' he said tightly.

'Lucas,' Ellie's mum said, with a bit more warmth than Ellie was comfortable with. 'What can I get you to drink?'

Ellie glared at her. Weren't they all meant to be being mean to Lucas? Her mother glared back. One of those multi-faceted glares that said, *This is the father of your child, child.* And, *This is long overdue, young woman.*

Humph.

She was thirty-five years old, not a stroppy teen!

Well. Perhaps she felt a little bit stroppy. Okay, very stroppy, but this was one of the moments she'd been avoiding for five years. The bigger one—the one where she explained to her son that he did have a father…

Sudden rushes of hot and cold swept through her. Five precious years she'd cared for and protected her boy, ensuring that, above all, he knew he was loved. Valued. Her parents adored him. Surprise, surprise. He was and would remain their only grandchild. His 'cool Uncle Drew' had been an awesome dad stand-in. Not on the romantic front because—*ew!*—she'd grown up with Drew and the idea of even— *Ew!* Not because he was icky looking. Quite the opposite, in fact, but…no. Her heart had always belonged to one man and one man only. Anyway, the point was that she had never wanted, for one solitary second, Maverick to think he was unwanted—like *some* people had made her feel. And now, with Lucas here, her son could very well turn the same accusatory look on her that Lucas had given her when he'd found he'd been denied five years of loving the world's most perfect little boy.

'A soft drink will be fine,' Lucas finally said.

Gordon gave a tight nod and went back behind the bar. 'I'll take it you'll have a wine, Ellie?'

She nodded and mouthed, 'Large, please.' She didn't normally drink on a 'school night' but…extenuating circumstances.

'Where's—?' Wyn began to ask, and then clapped her hands over her mouth.

'Don't worry, Mum. He knows.' Ellie flicked a look at Lucas who, to his credit, didn't launch into a high and mighty speech about Ellie's failure to tell him about Maverick.

Neither did he start telling her mum how she'd made him hide in the operating clinic while she'd extracted Maverick from the kennels without the promised show-and-tell session with the Uber-Vet. Or how he hadn't insisted on coming along when she'd escorted a very grumpy Maverick up to Henry's flat for an evening of spaghetti Bolognese and yet another showing of his favourite animated movie about pets.

He hadn't even brought up the topic of how she was going to run the clinic single-handedly when Henry left in the morning for London and she would, inevitably, try to make him leave again. Even the walk to the pub had been low maintenance. He'd pointed out a few things he thought had changed since he'd been down last—seven Christmases ago. He'd complimented her on the clinic—as well he should—and asked how they'd managed to create such an impressive facility on ten acres of prime real estate—with a lot of blue-sky thinking, some lottery funding, some private donations and the inclusion of a community petting zoo.

In all honesty, he'd been exactly like the Lucas she'd known six years ago minus the part about how they used to know everything about one another. Everything and then some. Her insides had been tingling from the moment she'd laid eyes on him. Still were.

'And here we are.' Gordon carried their drinks over to a quiet table at the back of the pub. It was a gorgeous evening so most of the customers were sitting on the picnic benches outside or in the small but pretty garden area behind the pub.

'So! Lucas,' her mother began. 'What brings you to town?'

Ellie was tempted to jump in but thought she'd leave this one to Lucas.

'The official reason is to replace Henry.'

'Oh?' Her mother threw her a questioning look.

Ellie parried the look to Lucas.

Lucas explained, 'My contract was up for renewal with the Uber-Vet, but I felt it was the right time to pass on the baton.'

Wyn spluttered her wine out. 'I thought that's what you wanted. The show.'

Lucas shot Ellie a look. One that asked why

on earth she hadn't explained the situation with his family to them.

Because her brain had pretty much exploded and been unable to receive more information when he'd told her he couldn't marry her any more, that's why. By the time she'd even begun to process what Lucas had been going through, she'd found out she was pregnant, and he had been appearing on the red carpet with another woman and…well…that was pretty much the story from then on.

'The show was a means to an end,' Lucas finally explained. 'My father's illness had put the clinic in a difficult financial position and my brother—'

'He's a vet, too, right?' Ellie's father asked.

'Yes. He…' A dark look shadowed Lucas's bright eyes. 'Jonty had his own problems to deal with, so…' He leant back in the booth and swept his fingers through his hair. 'Suffice it to say there were a lot of factors that led up to my decision to do the show and just as many to step away from it.'

One of the bar staff called out to her parents for some assistance. Ellie barely noticed them leave as a wave of understanding crashed through her.

Had Lucas been genuinely torn? She hadn't

been able to believe him. Proposing one day. Taking it back the next. Who *did* that?

But…maybe it hadn't been his decision at all. She desperately tried to remember exactly what Lucas had said to her that day.

There's been a change of plan. My priorities have changed. I don't want to drag you down with me.

She'd stopped listening then. The roar of blood blocking out everything else other than the fact that the love of her life had just dumped her.

But…had he?

There's been a change of plan.

She replayed the lines again.

I don't want to drag you down with me.

Had Lucas done the show because he'd *had* to?

The softening of her heart hardened. No. They'd been a couple. Deeply in love. When he'd proposed he had been prepared to announce to everyone they knew that he would be with her in sickness and in health, for richer, for poorer, all the terrible things— because weathering terrible things together made anything seem endurable. By pushing her to the side, he'd made it clear he hadn't trusted her to stick with him. That…that was the pain she'd born through the years.

Lucas scraped his crooked front tooth over his bottom lip, the blood draining from it as it dragged over the full, kissable mouth she'd never thought she'd lay eyes on again. Not in person anyway. The look he gave her said, *Please. Please give me a chance to explain.*

She gestured for him to continue.

'Since Dad died—'

'Wait! Your father passed away?'

'Didn't you know?' Lucas looked genuinely surprised.

'No. How would I—?' She stopped herself. It would've been in the papers. Or the veterinary magazines she subscribed to. 'I'm sorry. That must've been very difficult.'

Lucas nodded silently, his shoulders slumping as if reliving the weight of losing his father all over again.

'Is your mother all right?'

'She's better now.' His eyes shot to hers and in them she saw a wealth of pain.

Instinct kicked in and she pulled him into a quick tight hug and just as quickly pulled away. His scent, the familiarity of how they fitted together, his touch…it was all too much. She took a gulp of her wine then said hoarsely, 'How're you going to tell her about Maverick?' She dropped her head into her heads and moaned. 'Don't answer that. I don't have the slightest clue how to tell Mav that his TV hero is his father.'

'I'm his hero?' Lucas's expression lightened. The tension and pain dropped away from his features, leaving nothing but pure joy.

'Well,' she snipped. 'On television anyway.'

And then, completely unexpectedly, they shared a smile that reached into the very centre of her heart.

Dangerous? Absolutely.

Worth exploring?

Her brain threw that one back and forth for a second. Maybe for Maverick's sake. But only if Lucas were to meet about a hundred thousand criteria, including assuring her, beyond any reasonable doubt, that he would never, ever let her boy down.

Ellie's parents arrived back at the table just as Lucas took her hand in his and said, 'We need to talk.'

Wyn did an about face and turned her husband round with a cheeky smile. 'Darling? I think we might be needed in the kitchen.'

'Oh, right. Course.' Gordon gave the thick-slabbed table a knock. 'We'll leave you two lovebirds…erm…um…we'll leave you two to it. We'll be right behind the bar if you need anything.'

'What they need is to be alone, Gordo.' Wyn tugged him away from the table, lowering her voice as her gentle chiding continued.

Despite themselves, Ellie and Lucas both sniggered as Ellie's parents very indiscreetly tiptoed back to the kitchen and parked themselves at the pass, pretending not to stare at them.

'Excuse me.' A pair of tween-aged girls approached the table with white paper napkins in their hands, their parents sending them encouraging smiles from the far end of the pub. 'Would you mind signing our napkins? We just love your show.'

Lucas smiled and signed their napkins. The girls giggled and told him the names of all their pets and how Uber-Vet was, like, *totally* their favourite show. He tried to introduce them to Ellie, but it was clear they didn't really care who she was. They just wanted to talk to him, and it was easy to see why. He was warm, personable, and—*ha!*—he drew a little dog paw at the end of his signature. Adorable. Of course it was. Everything about him was perfect, except for the fact that when it had mattered most, he hadn't wanted her.

And just like that all the warm and fuzzy feelings percolating inside her evaporated. This wasn't a fairy-tale ending. It was the beginning of what would be a long, complicated emotional mess she'd be unravelling for years to come.

When they'd gone, Lucas leant in close to her. Goose-pimple close.

'Ells, do you think we could go somewhere a bit more private?'

Ellie arched an eyebrow. 'What? And deny your adoring fans a chance to meet the one and only Uber-Vet?'

Something hot fired in him and she knew she'd taken a step too far. Mocking him wasn't like her and while she might think of Lucas as many things, vain was definitely not one of them.

'I'd never begrudge the fans anything. The viewership kept my family from… I owe them a lot.' His eyes darkened with something she couldn't put a finger on and then that familiar smile softened them again as he rose from the bench seat. 'C'mon. We need to talk about this without an audience.'

She quickly told her parents they were going for a walk but that Lucas would need a room for the night. Her mum threw her one of those looks. *You'd better not mess this up, young lady. Your son deserves his father.*

Her stomach churned as they left the pub. Her mother's look was a blunt reminder that

Ellie wasn't entirely free to raise a flag on the moral high ground.

When they'd reached the beach path at the edge of the village, she turned to him. 'Why are you here, Lucas? Really?'

'Don't beat round the bush, Ells.' He laughed, then quickly corrected himself. 'Sorry. Ellie. Eleanor? Shall I call you Eleanor from now on?'

'No.' She gave him a play punch on the arm because after all the water under their particular bridge, using a formal name seemed ridiculous. 'But c'mon. Answer the question. Why are you really here? I doubt it's because you need the work.'

'No,' he said, much more seriously than she would've anticipated as their footsteps fell into a natural, matching stride. 'I want the work.'

She pursed her lips. 'Oh, c'mon, you're famous! You could work anywhere in the world. And you want to do a locum post in Dolphin Cove?'

He stopped and turned her to him, the heat in his hands easily filtering through her light linen top. 'I want to work with *you*. I never liked how we left things and a stupid part of me believed that if I came down…' He lifted his hands away and held them between them before she could interrupt him, her shoulders already feeling the loss of his touch. 'The plan wasn't exactly fully formed, but when Henry told me he was working here when I rang him a month back—'

'A month?'

Lucas nodded, looking as confused as she felt. 'Yeah. I rang him weeks ago to ask him to take over on the show. These things don't happen overnight.'

Ellie felt her jaw twitch. So it wasn't just her parents who'd wanted her to tell Lucas the truth. It was Henry. She knew Drew thought the same, though he'd never dared say as much. Was this the universe telling her she'd been wrong all of these years?'

'Ellie,' Lucas focused on her with an intensity that roared through her bloodstream, 'I am staying.'

She glared at him. It wasn't his call. It was hers!

Wasn't it?

The memory of *that day* surged back to the fore.

I don't want you being dragged down with me.

Had Lucas genuinely been trying to protect her from something? Ensuring she'd be free to follow her dreams? Why hadn't he seen that her dreams had included him?

He stood, silently, waiting. The man looked immovable. Gorgeously immovable. That. And he was the only vet in the country with enough skill to tackle the list of surgeries Henry had been scheduled to do.

'Oh, hell.' Her resistance faltered. 'It would be very useful if you could stay and work, but we need to figure out a plan with Maverick.'

'We?' He said, hope lighting up his eyes.

'Me,' she corrected. 'And your job will be to prove to me you respect my wishes. And my son's.'

Lucas nearly corrected her. Nearly said 'our son', then thought better of it. He would have his son in his life, and he'd take every step to ensure nothing got in the way of it. Even Mav's mama bear of a mum. She might be igniting all sorts of fires in him he'd long thought extinguished, but the one that burnt brightest… That flame burnt for his son.

At a split in the path, Ellie pointed him towards a sandy path edged with tall grasses. 'If we head off here, we can go to the beach in front of the clinic.'

'Beachfront property. That's quite a coup, Ellie.' He was impressed. 'I thought you and

Drew were going to set up in the village. Renovate an old shop.'

Ellie's eyebrows shot up in exactly the way Mav's had when he'd first spotted Lucas. 'No. The plan was that you, Drew and I were going to set up in the village. Drew and I decided to aim higher. Go for more of a community outreach angle.'

They rounded the corner into the idyllic cove where the veterinary clinic's windows shone in the ever-darkening hues of the remaining sunlight.

Ellie huffed out a sigh. 'Sorry. I'm being a pedant. You did your thing, we did ours. There's no need to stick the knife in.'

'It's me who owes you the apology, Ellie. Seriously. I know saying I left you in the lurch is a pretty massive understatement, but... I genuinely didn't feel as though I had a choice.'

'I got by,' she said in a voice that didn't sound entirely convinced.

He had too. Just. The bright lights and constant need to be 'in character' had never sat well with him. He loved being a vet. Plain and simple. He'd also loved Ellie every bit as much, but...he'd made what he had thought was the best choice. The only choice. Leaving his parents to battle debt and his father's debilitating disease on their own? He'd simply unable to do it. Not without dragging Ellie away from her dreams and her beloved Cornwall. The fact things had turned around so quickly with the Uber-Vet had seemed little short of divine intervention.

He opened his mouth to explain but clamped it shut, knowing anything he said on that front would only be digging himself a deeper hole.

What's done was done. The only thing he could do now was to look forward and the one thing he knew he'd have in his future was his son. No matter what Ellie thought.

Taking a step back from the heated emotions, Lucas opened his arms wide and turned away from the beach towards the clinic. 'You've done more than get by, Ells. Look at what you've accomplished. You've set up this incredible clinic, a surgical unit—'

'A petting zoo and a teaching centre,' Ellie said, a flush colouring her lightly tanned cheeks. A sense of accomplishment she clearly hadn't let herself feel added a couple more inches to her athletic five-foot-eight frame.

Without thinking, he reached out and gave her shoulder a rub, feeling her pride by proxy. For a nanosecond he felt her lean into his touch and then, as if it had never happened, the only thing he felt was the distance between them. 'You should be proud. You two have accomplished so much.'

The dark laugh that was so unlike her surfaced again. 'We probably would be in a crummy old shop if you hadn't dumped me.'

'What?' He made a noise indicating he doubted it. Not the Ellie he'd known anyway.

'We found a place in the village and it would've been perfectly fine, but when I found out about Mav there was no chance I was going to have him think he had a second-rate parent. If he ever found out about you, that is.'

Wow. There was a lot to unload in there. The last thing he would've ever said to his son was that he'd got a second-rate parent. Ellie was in her own class. An exemplary one.

Lucas felt as if she had reached inside his chest and crushed his own heart. He knew he'd hurt her. If he'd had any idea the pain had run this deep…

They stared at one another, their eyes searching each other's for answers to myriad questions until the atmosphere between them thickened. Lucas took a step forward. A bone-deep urge to pull her into his arms and promise her she'd never have to feel that harrowing pain again took hold of him, right up until a flat palm on the centre of his chest put a quick stop to that.

'We are going to discuss Mav and what to do about the fact you're his dad. And that's it.'

She was right. He had overstepped the mark but...hell's teeth. He would've done everything in his power to be with Ellie and Maverick if he'd known. Which did beg the follow-up question...why hadn't he wanted Ellie to be a part of his life as he'd untangled his family's almighty mess?

He'd thought he'd been protecting her. Plain and simple.

From the tiny acorn...grows the mighty oak.

After he'd proposed they'd gone on a walk. Soon enough they'd been laughing about all their hopes and dreams. Insane, considering they'd had no money, no clinic and zero clients. *Oh, well*, they'd said... *From the tiny acorn...* They'd stopped and kissed under an oak that must've been a good four hundred years old, vowing to leave a legacy of kindness and love in their wake that lasted as long as the tree.

That evening his father had rung and asked him to come home. Things, he'd said, weren't quite tickety-boo.

It had been the biggest understatement in the universe.

When he'd got there and learnt of the debt, the struggling clinic, his father's ever-increasing battle with Parkinson's and his AWOL older brother, it had been too much. He'd needed to focus. He'd not wanted to test the limits of their relationship—not when Ellie had had all the opportunities in the world.

As if reading his mind, she asked, 'Why wasn't I enough?'

'It wasn't you, honestly.'

Her eyes widened. 'You told me you loved me. You asked me to marry you. How could I have not taken it personally?' Before he could answer, she pointed at a log further down the beach. 'This isn't about you and me anymore. C'mon. Let's hash this out before I change my mind. Maverick is the priority here.'

'Absolutely,' Lucas said, swallowing down yet another lump of remorse into a gut already churning with discord. So much for a few weeks down in Cornwall making his peace then moving on with their lives. Ellie would be in his life for ever. It was up to the pair of them what form that relationship took. For his son's sake, he prayed it would be amicable.

'So!' She sat down on the log and tugged a hand through her curls, the sun lighting them in shades of fire and gold as if she were a Hollywood starlet. 'As you know from Henry, my *loyal* friend and colleague, Drew was in an awful car accident.'

Lucas nodded. He'd be stopping by to see him when time allowed. But his priority was to be here for Ellie and, as soon as possible, Maverick. 'I am happy to work all the hours you need.'

Ellie smirked. 'They're a lot longer than your fancy telly vet hours.'

He let that one slide. There was a lot more to it than swanning into an exam room, making a diagnosis then heading into surgery with a gaggle of nurses and vets in his wake. There had been planning meetings, research, actual vet work to ensure he was at the absolute top of his game, networking, scouting out difficult cases, media appearances with Katrina, and the list went on.

His father had helped with what he could but, in the end, his Parkinson's had got the better of him and soon even going through case files had been too exhausting. His death, whilst gut-wrenching, had meant he had no longer been in pain. His brother had resurfaced periodically, but after his father's death, a stint in rehab had been the only solution for his addiction. An expensive rehab clinic that had meant renewing the Uber-Vet contract again and chaining himself to a lifestyle in which he'd never felt entirely at home.

It had been worth it, though. His brother had found a small horse-centric clinic out in the countryside to practise in, joining Lucas and his mum for Sunday lunches to hash over difficult cases. Those meals had brought his family some much-needed peace. Enough for Lucas to finally say it was enough. It was time for him to live his own life now. So when his contract had come up for renewal? That was precisely what he'd done.

'Ellie.' Lucas shifted round on the log so that he was facing her. 'I know you think I'm different now, but for the most part I'm still the Lucas you met in vet school.' He held up a hand. 'I know you don't believe it and there are things I wish I could explain better than I did at the time.' He looked at Ellie, only to receive an eye-roll and a flick of the hand. She didn't want to hear it. Fine. It was painful terrain to hash over again and, just as he'd done all those years ago, he put the blinkers on again. But this time for his son. 'Are you happy for Maverick to know I'm his father?'

Ellie peered at him though her fingers. 'God, that's weird.'

'What?'

'Hearing you say Maverick's name. Seeing you take ownership of him as his father.'

Another well-aimed kick in the gut. She didn't trust him. Fair enough. He'd have to earn that too. And he would.

'I want to be his father, Ellie. I know there is no way I can make up for the years I've lost—but I can swear to you right now that I am going to do my damnedest trying.'

She gave him a look that echoed the mix of emotions he was experiencing. A mix of hope and fear. But mostly, *How can I believe you after you left me when it mattered most?*

He'd known the boy a matter of minutes, but primal instinct had lit a white-hot coil of connection in him. He'd sacrifice for Maverick. Protect. Honour. Cherish. Love. He was a father. He was Maverick's father and he'd do everything he could to ensure his little boy knew he was loved by both of his parents.

His own father had been a complicated man. Scientific. Dedicated to the animals he'd cared for. Close to his sons when he'd needed something. Like sacrifice. Distant when he hadn't. It had been the pain most likely. And pride. He had been a highly respected vet until Parkinson's had robbed him of his ability to perform surgery. Hobbled by his own body's frailty. It must've been a devastating blow to his pride.

Ellie stretched her legs out, her foot tracing an infinity pattern in the sand. It was the same pattern he'd had designed in diamonds for her engagement ring. The one she'd thrown at him when he'd told her he'd made a terrible mistake. 'I don't want him to hear a single lie.'

'No. Absolutely not,' he agreed.

'I don't want you making promises you can't keep.'

'I would never do that.'

She pursed her lips at him. He could almost feel the diamond ring bouncing off his chest as she whirled on one trendy trainered foot and out of his life. 'We'll see about that.'

Oh, she would. She'd see his commitment in spades.

They spoke about the logistics. Mav had surf school and science camp and also helped out at the vet's petting zoo, showing the other children that goats were fun to pet, and cows had scratchy tongues and no upper teeth. He liked to spend time with Torky, Tegan's twin, in the whelping unit during the socialisation hours and—she softened at this bit—nap time. School began again in September. He loved books so there would be lots of story-reading duties.

The list went on. Completely unlike the lists of duties that went with being the Uber-Vet, Lucas was loving each and every detail. His respect for Ellie also went up a significant notch. 'How do you do all of it? Motherhood and running the clinic.'

She shrugged. 'It's hard, but Mum and Dad are amazing. Drew's a brilliant uncle and, well, pretty much the whole village has helped because they all want their animals looked after and the only way that happened in the early years was if Mav came along.'

'You took him with you?'

'I didn't have much choice, did I?' Their eyes clashed and held.

Choice.

What a loaded word.

She'd not given him a choice. Not even a chance to offer help. Then again, he'd not given her a choice either. Not much of a leg to stand on in the self-righteous department. So he stayed quiet, his frustration humming through him in sharp bursts filled with static.

'Here's how I see it playing out,' Ellie continued officiously. 'If, and only if, Maverick takes the news well, you can stay the eight weeks the clinic needs you. After that?' She gave her head a little shake. 'We'll see.' She flicked her thumb over her shoulder towards the flat she and Mav shared. 'Tonight you're staying at the Pelican. I'm sure my mother has a million more questions for you. After that, whilst I'm not entirely thrilled about this, it makes more sense for you to move into the staff flat. I've been doing most of the night duty calls.'

He looked at her through fresh, professional eyes. She looked tired. The strain, no doubt, of taking up the slack whilst her partner recovered from his accident. Something tugged at his heart that he'd tamped down in order to get through his own trials. Compassion. Empathy.

'That's a lot of work for one person, Ellie.'

She scrubbed a hand over her face. 'Yup. Well. We're a young business trying to make a big mark. I normally take Mav to my mum, but it'd be nicer for him not to be woken up, so I'll wake you up instead. Welcome to parenthood!' She briskly began to rattle off more details—Mav's favourite pyjamas, how he liked his pillows, which were his favourite cuddly toys. 'He doesn't like marshmallows in his hot chocolate and is scared of the dark, so don't ever, ever turn off the small lamp on top of his chest of drawers.' She rubbed the heel of her hand against her bare knee, the edges of her A-line skirt fluttering in the light sea breeze. 'And he likes your show.' She threw him a soft smile.

'Why, Ellie Stone. Is that a compliment?'

'No.' She pushed herself up to stand to avoid his gaze. 'Just a fact.'

Speaking of facts... 'What did you tell him about his father? About me?'

She shrugged. 'Nothing much. Just that I loved him and not everyone had a daddy on the scene—a bit like the animal kingdom. You know, daddy lions don't hang around to teach baby lions how the world works because they have prey to stalk. Territory to protect.'

He snorted. Trust Ellie to use lions to explain why mummies hung around and daddies didn't. Then again, it was a fairly apt analogy. Ellie had created an amazing 'den' here. A place to care, protect and feed her son. And all the while Lucas had been protecting her. Not that she saw it that way, but...one day. Maybe one day. Miracles did happen. Like this one. He had a son. A beautiful boy by an equally beautiful mother who, one day, might forgive him for having turned his back on her when he'd thought he'd had no other choice.

She clapped her hands together. 'So! Let's

go and rip the plaster off, shall we? Then you
can hoof it back to Mum and Dad. Mav'll
have a lot of questions and we both have a
long day tomorrow.'

Walking behind her as she briskly made
her way up to the clinic, Lucas realised he
was smiling. An entirely new life was about
to begin for him and, unlike the time he'd shut
himself off from his own ambitions, this time
he couldn't wait to start. Bring it on. Bring
it all on.

CHAPTER FOUR

MAVERICK STARED AT Ellie then Lucas then back at Ellie. 'For real?'

Ellie nodded, still a bit shell-shocked herself. She'd just told her son who his father was.

Maverick crossed his legs underneath his endangered animals duvet cover, briefly making the tiger's head look as if it were surging forward to take a bite out of someone. Lucas, preferably. Her son turned his blue-eyed gaze on her. 'I thought you said my daddy was a pirate.'

Ellie's cheeks burnt at the memory. She'd said it on a whim once, never for a second thinking he'd believe her, but...it was how she thought of Lucas sometimes. A swashbuckling love thief. *Stick with the facts, Ellie!* 'Nope. 'Fraid not, love. He's a vet.'

'The Uber-Vet,' Maverick said in a reverent

tone, his gaze swinging back to Lucas. 'It's like…it's like… I am *made* of vets!'

Lucas grinned from the foot of the bed where Ellie had made him sit amongst the jumble of cuddly toys. As annoying as it was to have her son all googly-eyed over the fact his father was the Uber-Vet, it was nice to see Mav take the news on board as easily as he accepted being pulled out of bed and slipped into her mother's spare room while she went off to check on a colicky horse or attend a late-night calving. Would that she had taken the news her engagement would only last twenty-four hours with such ease.

Mav popped his elbow onto his knee and his chin into his hand as he stared at Lucas for a moment. 'I suppose we do have the same earlobes.'

Ellie couldn't help herself. She cracked up. Earlobes! They had a lot more than that in common. Eyes. Hair. Dry wit—yes, even at five. And a brain that never stopped whirring with curiosity.

'Are you going to move in with us?' Mav asked Lucas.

Gulp. Case in point.

'Oh, now… I think your daddy…' Crikey, that had felt strange. Saying 'daddy' with Maverick's actual daddy sitting there. Did he even want to be called Daddy? 'Lucas will staying at the Hungry Pelican tonight.'

'But I'll be moving in next door tomorrow,' Lucas said reassuringly to Mav, and then, conciliatory to Ellie, 'To make things easier for Mummy when she's on night calls.'

Mummy.

Oh, jeepers. Who knew hearing that out of Lucas's mouth would give her butterflies? To ignore them she countered with a cheery, 'Unless, of course, Mummy decides to send Daddy on the night call.'

Ellie and Lucas shared a little tug-of-war smile. It reminded her of when they'd gone out on an internship at a huge clinic up north together when, in the dead of winter, they'd used to play rock, paper scissors to decide who went out to do a midnight calving or a pre-dawn set of lamb triplets where the farmer would, inevitably, surprise the vet with a series of 'While I have you here...' cases in their huge, unheated barns. The butterflies took flight again.

'So...' Maverick gave his curly mop a scratch. 'Will I stay in my bed?'

'Absolutely.' Ellie sent a pointed look in Lucas's direction but refused to meet his eyes. How did a man who'd crushed her heart to bits manage to warm the cockles of that very same heart with one cheeky grin? She took Maverick's hands in hers and began to play pat-a-cake with them. 'I will be in my bed. And your daddy will stay in his bed. Next door.'

'But...don't daddies live with mummies?' Maverick asked.

Ellie could feel Lucas's eyes on her. The butterflies hummed with excitement. Would she like Daddy to live with Mummy? Her body obviously would, but her brain was shouting out the reminder that daddies didn't get to just pop up after six years of absence and pretend they hadn't kicked Mummy to the kerb right after they'd proposed to her. She blew out a little breath before she answered. 'Daddies and mummies who haven't seen each other in a while sometimes have different ways of living.'

'You mean like Rockford and Esmerelda?'

'Who're they?' Lucas asked.

'The stud dog and Mum's golden retriever.'

'Ah,' said Lucas, glints of humour sparking in his eyes and then quickly going out as he put two and two together.

Ellie bit the inside of her lip. Lucas had given her Esmerelda along with a promise to love her until the day she died.

Lucas gave his stubbly chin a rub then said

to Mav, 'Yes. I suppose you could compare our situation to that.'

'But Rockford has lots of lady friends.' Maverick began listing them off. It was one of his hobbies. Keeping track of all of the 'lady friends' Rockford had. Perhaps this hadn't been the best of analogies.

Ellie turned to Lucas, interested to see how he handled this one. Definitely a daddy question.

He spluttered for a moment then said, 'True, true. But he also has all sorts of puppies he never gets to spend time with. Or read stories to. I'd like to be able to do that, so I guess I am a bit different from Rockford…' He looked up and met Ellie's eyes. 'I'm a one-woman kind of stud dog.'

Oh, boy. There was so much to unpack from that. So she looked at the clock and announced, 'Bedtime! Unless you have any more questions?'

'No,' Maverick said, snuggling down under his light summer duvet. 'Since I have eight weeks to ask questions, I can put them in my book. Next to your autograph. That way I will always have a record that you were real.'

Tears instantly sprang to Ellie's eyes. He'd already prepared for Lucas to leave. When she heard Lucas clear his throat, she knew her son's statement had hit him right in the solar plexus as well.

Lucas scooched round on the bed until he was sitting right behind Ellie—as if they were a happily married couple who always sat without as much as a hair's breadth between them.

'You'll never have to worry about that, son. I'll always be here for you. Whenever you need me.'

Ellie looked away, trying to make it look like the tears she was wiping away were actually some unfortunate specks of dust in her eyes.

'You just keep the questions coming. Okay?'

Maverick squinted at Lucas for a moment and then asked, 'Do you think our earlobes are the same?'

Lucas gave his hand a squeeze and tucked a stuffed polar bear, Maverick's favourite, into the crook of his little boy's arm. 'Identical,' he said, then leant down and gave his son a kiss on the forehead before getting up to leave. 'I'll let you and your mum have a bit of alone time, yeah?

'Okay, Dad,' Maverick said, as easily as if he'd been calling Lucas 'Dad' from the day he could speak. 'And in the morning I'll introduce you to Esmerelda. She's got ten perfect pups! Mummy says it's because she was a perfect match to Rockford.'

Lucas winked at Maverick then at Ellie. 'Your mother always did have good taste in men.' And just like that Ellie fell a little bit back in love with Lucas Williams who, despite everything she'd done to forget him, was still very, very real.

Lucas was a complicated mix of fidgety and delighted. He'd slept poorly, had gone for a run along the beach but had been expressly forbidden from turning up at the clinic until it opened so he'd filled in some more time by taking up Wyn's offer of a hot breakfast.

At least he knew now that Ellie's parents didn't view him as the enemy. Quite the opposite, in fact. After being hammered with twenty questions about the show—it was rewarding to raise the profile of animal welfare—his future work plans—to stay here in Dolphin Cove until something new surfaced—his late father—missed, but at peace—his mother—reinventing herself as a charity event doyenne—and his brother—living a quiet life in the Cotswolds—Lucas pushed back his plate and gave Wyn a smile.

'That was an incredible English breakfast.'

'Cornish,' she briskly corrected him. 'You won't be getting hog's pudding or Cornish potato cakes up in London, I expect.'

'No. Good point.' He'd be drinking ginger and turmeric smoothies and whatever other ghastly things the craft services truck had supplied to keep him 'camera-ready'. This, he realised, was one of the first proper meals he'd eaten sitting at a table that wasn't a business meeting.

'Neither do you get women the quality of my Ellie, I would think,' Wyn said, eyes trained on him like a hawk's. 'Up there in London.'

Lucas smiled. Okay. So it was sort of a business meeting. 'Very true. She is one of a kind.'

Wyn sat back in her chair, eyes still glued to him as she took a long draught of her tea. 'Six long years,' she said when she had finished. 'I suppose you could've gone and got married yourself in that time.'

His jaw tightened. Nope. There'd just been the one proposal. He'd had a couple of girl-friends over the years, but after the debacle with Ellie he'd vowed never to propose to anyone again. Life threw too many curve-balls to make that mistake twice. As such, girlfriends hadn't lasted long. That and the sixteen-hour workdays.

'Oh, no, Mrs. Stone. It's been all work and no play for me, I'm afraid.'

'Wyn,' she corrected him, more gently, he supposed now that she knew he hadn't run off and married someone else. She gave him a pat on the knee and picked up his plate, preparing to head back to the kitchen. He might not have retained number one almost-son-in-law status, but he'd always remembered her saying how important it was never to hold a grudge.

Too many to carry around, she said, *by the time you hit fifty. Who needs extra weight when gravity is already against you?*

'Wyn,' he repeated, grateful for the olive branch.

She narrowed her gaze at him. Here it was. The sting after the sweetening. 'Tell me, Lucas. Why are you here?'

He trotted out his line, knowing it would never be enough. 'Henry said Ellie needed help and I—'

Wyn cut him off. 'Ellie and Drew have needed help ever since they started the clinic. It was meant to be a three-person surgery…' She tapped the side of her nose. 'If memory serves.'

'Yes. Yes, it was.'

She waved in a couple who were peering into the pub, asking after coffees. 'Grab a table and I'll bring the menus over in a second.' Then to Lucas, 'I don't want you telling me anything you haven't told my Ellie yet, but know this—you broke that girl's heart clean through. Don't let her convince you otherwise. The boy of hers, my grandson, is the most precious thing in the world to her. I'm not a woman who issues threats because there's enough hate in the world, but if you hurt one single hair on either my baby girl or my grandson's head…'

'I know, Mrs Stone. I wish I could explain everything, but…'

I wanted to keep Ellie safe. Out of my family's black hole of debt.

Wyn tutted. 'Actions speak louder than words, sonny boy. Actions.'

She was right. Actions did. He'd pushed Ellie aside exactly when the marriage vows he'd never taken had told him he should've pulled her close. Because of that he'd missed the first five years of his son's life.

Like it or not, it was time to re-examine his view on life. He kissed Wyn's cheek and followed it with a solemn smile. 'Guess I'd better start making up for lost time.'

Wyn returned his sober smile. 'I'd guess you'd better.' She tapped her watch face. 'Time's a tickin'.'

Through the small crowd of pet owners arriving for their early appointments, Lucas saw the familiar red gold hair up at Reception and then, as if she sensed him approaching, Ellie lifted her green eyes to meet his.

A zap of connection instantly lit up his nervous system. It felt like being alive again. Properly, completely alive for the first time in…years really. As if part of his heart had died the day he'd told her he had to walk away. Not that he was being all *Boo-hoo, poor me* about this. He'd made the decision and he'd stuck to it. His family was back on track, he'd paid forward the benefits of the show to the veterinary college and now it was time to make amends to the one woman who lit him up from the inside out.

He'd hurt her. He had to own that.

Did the fact she'd kept Maverick a secret burn? No doubt about it. He'd lain awake half the night wishing Ellie had told him. Used the anger she felt for him to present herself on set with what had no doubt been a gorgeous big old pregnant belly and said, *This is yours, pal. Own it.*

Bah. He wouldn't have wanted to raise his son in that household during those first three years and he hardly could've left his parents. It had been one of those times when life had slung everything at a man just to see what he was made of. Stronger stuff than he'd thought, but...*damn*...had he been strong enough to have also raised a child amidst all that chaos?

Clipboard in hand, glasses perched on her nose, Ellie gave him a quick smile that didn't exactly exude warmth, but she wasn't telling him to leg it back to London either. Part of the deal, he supposed, when she'd promised her son eight weeks with the father he'd never known.

'So!' He strode up to the counter intent on putting his best foot forward. 'What's on the roster today?'

'Hi, Lucas.' Tegan was beaming at him, half-sprawled across the high reception counter as she threw him a long-limbed wave. Ellie ignored her.

'Morning,' he said to Tegan, then to Ellie, 'Want to run me through the day's list?'

'What? Like one of your producers?' She put on a fancy London voice. 'Well, Mr Uber-Vet...today we have a variety of delights for you to ease yourself in here at Dolphin

Cove Clinic.' She held her clipboard at arm's length and ran her finger dramatically down it. 'Let's see. Your first patient is Rufus.' She looked up at him with a bright smile. 'His anal glands need cleaning.'

Ha! That was normally a job for the vet nurses. And usually pretty stinky. Fair enough. She was testing him. He gave her a 'bring it on' smile. Another zap of connection flashed between them. A reminder of the fun they'd had when they'd interned together. Daring each other to do more and more difficult diagnoses whilst mastering the basics. They had brought out the best in each other. Maybe one day they could do it again.

'Ells! Anal glands?' Tegan was looking at her in horror. 'That's no way to treat our guest. Get Mum to do it.'

'Mum?' Lucas asked.

'My mum's the senior vet nurse here,' Tegan explained officiously, as if she and not Ellie was in charge of the clinic. 'She does all that kind of stuff. Plus laser treatment, dressing changes. She's amazeballs. Ellie! Give him something pukka. The man doesn't want boring.'

Ellie gave her a bright smile. 'Nope. He's an employee. We're all created equal here.'

'Okay…' Tegan rolled her eyes melodramatically. 'Looks like *someone* woke up on the wrong side of the bed.' Before Ellie could protest, Tegan smiled and waved at a harried-looking woman being pulled into the clinic by an enthusiastic Rottweiler. 'I'll just check Mrs Collins in, shall I?'

Ellie handed Lucas the clipboard that held a list of the day's patients and their complaints. He gave it a quick scan.

There were a surprising number of anal glands to be seen to today.

He tried to hide his smirk with a serious look but failed.

'Sounds good.' Snigger.

'You think blocked anal glands are funny?' Ellie asked.

'Not in the slightest.'

Their eyes clashed and held. What was really going on here? Was this Ellie's way of fighting an attraction that obviously hadn't died or was she trying to bore him into leaving?.

He put himself int her shoes. Realistically? This must be an epic nightmare. Well. Too bad. He had a son to think about now. He held her gaze with a look he hoped said, *I'm staying, darlin'. Anal glands or no anal glands.*

Tegan finished with the woman she was checking in then looked between the pair of them. 'What was that? Did you two just share a look?'

Ellie gave her a scarcely veiled side eye. 'No. I don't even know what that means. *A look*. Pfft.'

Tegan's face lit up with a naughty smile. 'I just remembered. Lucas…you and Ellie used to date at uni, didn't you?'

That was one way to put it. He was just about to leave it to Ellie to put her spin on things when Maverick ran in, boogie board under his arm and a beagle running behind him.

'Mum! I'm off to surf school.' He stopped when he clocked Lucas. 'Hi, Dad!'

'Dad?' Tegan's jaw almost dropped to the counter.

Ellie gave her a tight little smile. 'Yes, well…'

'Ooh.' Tegan was relishing this. Big time. 'You are a dark horse, Ellie. A very dark horse indeed.'

'Maybe I'd better start seeing patients.' Lucas said, easing himself away from the reception desk, ruffling his hand through Lucas's hair as he did so.

Maverick beamed up at him then said, 'Don't forget. You said you'd come with me to the whelping unit before lunch.'

Lucas gave him a nod and a salute. 'Wild horses wouldn't keep me away.'

'Actually,' Ellie began, 'there are some wild ponies out on the moor about twenty miles away. Someone rang in this morning to say she thought one had a bad cut on its forehead. Catching them could be tricky. Might take hours.'

'Oh?' Lucas quirked an eyebrow. He'd not had to round up an animal in ages. Years really. Could be interesting. More interesting than anal glands, anyway.

'Ellie!' cried Tegan, who clearly didn't want Lucas to leave Reception let alone the clinic.

'Mum!' cried Maverick, who had obviously been banking on puppy time.

She threw up her hands.

'Fine! We'll do the ponies together once we've finished with morning surgery, but you...' she pointed at Lucas '...had better get cracking. We'll leave after you've spent time with Mav and the puppies.'

Lucas gave his jaw a scrub and nodded. Actions spoke louder than words and he wasn't above eating a bit of humble pie. He rubbed his hands together and grinned. 'Right. Point me to an exam room and I'll get started. Rufus? Is Rufus Collins here?'

The woman with the Rottweiler lurched forward as the dog bounded towards Lucas. 'Oh, my days,' cried the woman. 'It's the Uber-Vet! Rufus, look! You're going to have a celebrity see to your stinky bot-bot.'

With a huff of irritation, Ellie called her first patient and headed towards her exam room with a pair of chihuahuas in tow.

With a slight bow Lucas led the way into his exam room across the corridor. It was going to be a long day but a fun one.

'Ring me *any time* if you're worried, all right?' Ellie put her patient, a tiny budgie with a cyst under its wing, back into its cage. She ushered the owner out with a gentle suggestion to ease back on the 'free-range flying' sessions in the conservatory. Flying into crystal-clear windows had caused the ruptured air sac and, whilst it would heal, more incidents wouldn't be in the bird's favour. With a smile and wave, she went back into the exam room, aware of the low murmurs and laughter coming from the exam room Lucas was using.

Irritation crackled through her. Everyone seemed to be having a gay old time across the hall, whereas on her side grumpiness had definitely been the order of the day.

She gave her shoulders a bit of a jiggle. This was happening whether she liked it or not. There was no turning back time or changing the facts. Her son knew his father and his father wanted to stay.

For the next eight weeks, she briskly reminded herself as another gale of laughter erupted from his exam room.

She resisted the urge to press her ear to the door to try and figure out what they were talking about. The pet? His show? Her?

Bleurgh. What did it matter? They were all under the spell of the gorgeously perfect Uber-Vet.

Funny how no one remembered the lanky, goofier-looking version of Lucas who had come down to Dolphin Cove a handful of times over the course of their training. The nerdy animal geek who had yet to grow into his six-foot-two frame, figure out a haircut that worked for him and... *Hee-hee*. She started to giggle. The glasses! How could she forget the glasses he used to wear? Thick, tortoiseshell frames he'd thought had made him look studious and French.

She leaned against the wall, the memory of him pretending to speak in French whilst waving his glasses around in an erudite fashion tipping her smile ever upwards.

The door opened and Lucas was there, tall and gorgeous. No glasses. Those bright blue eyes of his hit hers with a heat so direct she could almost feel it. 'You all right?'

'Mmm…' she said, a bit too aware of the warm vibrations the sound produced.

Oh, Lucas, she thought. *Why have you come back? What do you* really *want?*

It terrified her to think the answer might be her. Equally scary was the possibility it wasn't.

Mrs Cartwright and Tabatha appeared from behind his exam-room door.

Ellie's smile dropped away.

'Mrs Cartwright? Lucas saw Tabatha yesterday and she was fine. Has something happened?'

Mrs Cartwright threw her a guilty look then leant a little more heavily on the arm Lucas has proffered her. 'It's ever so nice having a proper gentleman in the surgery, dear, isn't it?'

Humph!

She didn't think Henry or Drew would be very pleased with that pronouncement. It did suggest Tabatha was still in fine fettle but… Mrs Cartwright was looking a bit frailer. Ellie worried that her only human contact was with the vets here at the clinic, so…if she wanted to add Lucas to her list, fair enough. She'd have to brace herself for heartbreak in, oh, about seven weeks and four days. Not that she was making big fat Xs on her mental calendar or anything.

'Why don't we get you a packet of those special treats for Tabatha I was telling you about?' Lucas said as he slowly escorted her down the corridor. 'They'll definitely help with her digestion.'

Smoothie, Ellie thought, primly marching herself back to her exam room to finish up her notes. Her phone began to buzz on the countertop. Drew.

Interesting. She'd been the one ringing him over the past few weeks. Not that she blamed him for withdrawing from the world for a bit. The poor guy had been hit by several emotional hammer blows over the past couple of years, not to mention the physical ones. First his fiancée died in a tragic accident and now he'd bashed his leg into smithereens after a catastrophic brake failure in his car. Maybe this call was a sign he'd begun to turn the corner. Or it could just be that he was happy to be in his own house again. Several months of hospital food didn't sound that fabulous.

'Hey, there, friend,' she said, lodging the phone against her shoulder whilst typing in the final instructions for Biddy the Budgie's dressing. 'How's the leg?'

'A little birdie tells me Henry has left for the dazzling lure of Hollywood.'

Ellie heaved out a sigh. So much for casual chitchat. 'Yup. Well. London-wood. I should've rung, but things have been a bit crazy.'

'Crazy in what way?' Drew asked in a way that made it very clear that the birdie had also told him Lucas was there.

'Lucas came in to replace him.'

'Huh,' said Drew in his characteristically dry way.

'Exactly.'

'And has he—?'

'Yes. He's met Maverick. He figured it out. And we told him. About Maverick, I mean.'

'Strewth, woman. You don't mess around.'

'Well, it's pretty difficult to disguise the fact that they're related. And, yes, I did try to hide Maverick, but Torky told him the Uber-Vet was in Reception and—'

'Mav came running,' Drew finished for her.

'Yup.'

'Need a shoulder to cry on? I've got some double chocolate salted caramel ice cream.'

'I'd love both of those things,' Ellie said,

'but sadly I have a clinic to run, a son to raise and…' She sniggered.

'What?'

'I told Lucas the ponies out on the moor were wild.'

'What?' He guffawed. 'You're naughty. They'd do everything friendly apart from brush your hair for you.'

'I know, I just…' She tugged her hair out of its ponytail. 'I just wanted…' What *did* she want?

'Him to feel as much of an idiot as you did?'

'Don't mince your words or anything, Drew,' she said, and then wailed, 'It's just not fair! It'd be easier if I wanted revenge or thought he was revolting or—

'Wait. You still have the hots for him?'

'No!' she shouted. Too fast. Too hotly. *Oh, hell*. She still had the hots for him. Not very useful in the whole build a cage around her heart plan.

'Let's back up a minute here.' Drew took a couple of loud, yoga-style breaths. 'Now. Let's start over. What is it you want while Lucas is here for the remainder of my purgatory?'

'You could start doing more of your exercises.'

'Uh-uh,' Drew tutted. 'We're talking about your problems, not mine.'

Ellie harrumphed. 'Well…revenge is out because it's not like I'm going to propose to him and then take it back.' Or that he would even accept. She couldn't read him as well as she used to be able to. Maybe he genuinely was here to help out at the clinic and that was it. Except…now that he knew he had a son, everything was different.

'I don't know,' she sighed. 'It's complicated. If there hadn't been a Lucas there wouldn't be a Maverick and as we know…'

Drew joined in with her, 'Maverick is the best little boy in the West.' And he was. She wouldn't trade one ounce of the heartache she'd endured if it meant losing her son, but… this whole father appearing out of the blue thing would be a lot easier to deal with if she felt nothing when she looked at Lucas.

Drew broke into her silent reflection. 'What do the clients think of having the Uber-Vet at their beck and call?'

Ellie had to laugh. 'They love it. Mrs Cartwright's been in.'

'Surprise, surprise.'

'Twice in two days,' she clarified.

'Ah,' there was a note of concern in Drew's voice. 'Are we to worry about Tabatha?'

'No. I think we need to put the kettle on a bit more frequently for Mrs Cartwright, though.'

'Smart. And how's Esmerelda's litter coming along?

'Brilliant. They're all genius puppies.'

Drew laughed. 'Of course they are. I'd expect nothing less.'

'Want one?'

'No.'

'Sure?'

'Yes.'

'How's physio going?'

'Can we change the topic, please, Ells?'

There was a sharp note to Drew's voice Ellie didn't like. 'I'm going to pop one of Mum's lasagnes by tonight.' Even though he was home, she doubted he was hobbling round the house enough to cook.

'I'm fine.'

'You love her lasagne.'

'And you have enough on your plate without fussing about me. Go see the patients. I can hear them howling in the background.'

He couldn't, but he did have a point. The clinic had a gazillion bookings. 'Right you are, my friend. I'll leave you to it, but call me if you need anything, all right? Otherwise I'll sic Mav on you.'

'Ooh. My worst nightmare!'

Ellie signed off with a smile. Cool Uncle Drew was a lifesaver when it came to Mav. More than that, he was family, minus the DNA. He'd been the one to get her boy on a surfboard at the ripe old age of three. The one who'd been with her when he'd taken his first steps. Got his first tooth. Announced he was going to be a vet, just like them...*and* the Uber-Vet. The look they'd shared over Maverick's head when he'd come out with that one...it had been a doozy.

Ellie went out to the central reception desk and grinned. Everyone was talking, petting animals that weren't theirs, discussing summer plans and whether or not they'd change because of Fluffy's cone of shame or Patch's paw in plaster. Every day was different, but she was pretty sure that having Lucas around brought this extra level of wattage to the clinic's waiting room.

Whilst it was mildly irritating that everyone who came to see her asked, for the first time ever, if she was really sure about her diagnosis and maybe they should get Lucas in for a second opinion, she also knew everyone who did see him was in good hands.

One thing she knew for sure about Lucas Williams was that he was a good vet.

Just as well given that everything else was up in the air.

After a busy morning of seeing numerous cats, dogs and a ferret, Ellie headed out to the van to make sure it was all kitted out for the on-site calls they had lined up next, including the wild pony. Once she'd done her check she headed off to find her son who would no doubt be starving after surf school.

She quietly eased opened the door to the puppy unit and instantly felt the air leave her lungs.

There, sitting amongst the pile of snoozing pups was her son, curled up on a lamb's wool rug, asleep, with two puppies snuggled up close. Sitting next to them, eyes also closed, puppy in one hand, the other gently resting on Mav's leg, was Lucas.

If she could erase the past six years and re-write them, this was one of many moments she would've written in. Absolute perfection. Despite herself, she tugged her phone out of her pocket and took a photo. For Maverick, obviously.

Lucas's eyes opened at the shutter sound. When they lit on Ellie he smiled exactly the type of smile she should be resisting if she didn't want her heart broken all over again.

He eased himself out of the tangle of puppies and little-boy limbs and joined her at the edge of the pen. 'He's a credit to you.'

The both looked at Maverick, pride swelling in both of their chests. Ellie was struck by what a 'proud parents' moment it was. Something she definitely should not get used to. Lucas might be all about staying now but he hadn't been through a tired little boy tantrum. Or an 'eat your vegetables' standoff. He'd tire of it soon enough. Wish himself back into his old life.

'We should get going.' She went to get Maverick but Lucas beat her to it. More deftly than she would've imagined, he scooped their little boy up into his arms, his head nestling into Lucas's shoulder, exactly where she'd used to snuggle when they had been watching a film or a bit of telly in between study sessions.

'Where do we take him?'

Ellie pointed to the flat. 'Tegan's mum, Cardy, is up there. She'll be there for him when he wakes up and get him some lunch. After that he'll go to my parents'. They're having a board games afternoon at the pub and Maverick has got a jigsaw puzzle on the go.'

Something passed across Lucas's eyes she couldn't quite put her finger on. Remorse? Respect? A mix of both? It was hard to say.

Once he'd tucked Mav into his bed, they tiptoed out of the flat.

'Right,' Ellie said with as bright a smile as she could muster. 'Ready for some cowboy action?'

CHAPTER FIVE

LUCAS PULLED OFF his long glove, wiped his brow and smiled. 'I've never done that before.'

'Seriously? No breech alpaca births in London?' Ellie held out a bag for him to put the gloves in, popped it to the side then took a deep drink from her water bottle, a trendy reusable number with the clinic's logo on it. It was a hot summer's day with only a hint of a sea breeze as they were a few acres inland at Viola's farm, the very aptly named Seaview Farm.

'Nope. Not on my watch anyway.' Lucas leaned against the fence, in awe as the newly born alpaca tried, then succeeded in standing up on his reedy little legs. 'I would say this entire week has been filled with quite a few firsts.'

Ellie threw him a look.

Seeing each other for one.

Learning he had a son for another.

Then finding a weird but strangely work-able routine over the past week where, be-tween the two of them, they looked after Mav. More accurately, Ellie showed him how par-enting worked whilst keeping her own feel-ings about things hidden.

Despite the little flashes and flares of frus-tration that crackled between them, he liked to think he was settling into the groove of things. He willingly dived into getting Mav sorted for surf class or science camp or sup-per or bedtime. Making sure he had enough puppy time, nap time and brushed his teeth. Genuine, honest to goodness, quality time.

It didn't mean it was all footloose and fancy free. He hadn't missed Ellie's odd aside about Maverick still being in awe of the fact that his father was the Uber-Vet so was on his best be-haviour. She couldn't wait to see how he han-dled things when Mav had a tantrum in the middle of the supermarket or refused to brush his teeth or, God forbid, came down with any-thing, because Maverick was many things, but a good patient was not one of them.

'Chickenpox,' she'd whispered. 'You were lucky you missed it.'

'No,' he'd retorted. 'I regret having missed it. That and so much more.'

Not that he'd had much time to wallow in a sea of regrets. The clinic was a constant hive of activity. Very different from the specialised work he'd been focussing on to keep the show's ratings up. The Dolphin Cove Veterinary Clinic was half animal hospital, half community centre. It made sense seeing the place had largely been built from local crowd funding. And, of course, it made sense when you knew Ellie. She loved people every bit as much as she loved animals. And she loved animals a lot.

They'd caught the wild pony in the end. Turned out all you had to do was walk up to it with a carrot. Ellie had let him think otherwise for just a little bit too long on that front. Never mind. There were worse hurdles she could throw in his path. Like refusing to let him have access to Maverick. One week in and his heart had shown an elasticity he'd not believed it capable of. He loved his little boy more than he had ever imagined loving anyone…anyone apart from Ellie. Not that he was free to 'go there' any more. That chapter was well and truly finished. A niggle surfaced. Was it? Could he change his own rules?

Ellie took another drink of water and handed him her bottle. 'Here. Hydrate.' She inspected him for a minute. 'I would've thought you'd have seen every animal under the sun by now.'

'You didn't ever really watch the show, did you?' He handed back the bottle, catching Ellie's eyes observing him as he eased out the kinks from the awkward way he'd had to stand during the birth of the cria. He pretended he didn't see the flush hit her cheeks. 'Cats and dogs were our bread and butter cases. They're more relatable.' She nodded for him to continue. 'We had a python who'd swallowed a football, but wisely brought in a specialist herpetologist.' He ticked off some more animals. 'Ferrets, tortoises, mice and hamsters have made the odd showing. Goats, cows, horses, pigs, but nope. No alpacas.'

Ellie gave him a grin, her golden curls swishing across her shoulders. 'Well. Now you can tick that off your list.'

He folded into a courtly bow. 'Much obliged to you, m'lady. Got any tigers hidden away anywhere?' His eyes flicked up to meet hers. The heat in her cheeks doubled.

'Not unless you count the beast of Bodmin Moor,' she answered loftily.

'Ah…the fabled Beast of Bodmin. Whatever happened to it, I wonder.'

'Probably waiting for the Uber-Vet to show up so it could make a splash on telly.'

Ouch. The jibes weren't frequent, but when Ellie made one, he felt it.

'Ha-ha.' He nudged her with his elbow then turned serious. Finding out he had a son mustn't detract from the fact he had originally come down here to make amends. 'I'm not all about the bright lights big city you know.'

Ellie looked at him. Hard. She swallowed as if she was choking back something not very nice to say then gave a nonchalant shrug. 'I guess.'

Lucas took another swig of water from Ellie's bottle. 'Mmm… Good. Better than the water in London.' It was the closest he could come to saying that he wished things had turned out differently.

'Everything in Cornwall is better than London,' Ellie said with a cheeky grin.

'Ha! That's quite a statement.'

'She's not wrong,' a firm, posh voice cut in. 'Air's better. Sea's cleaner. Sun's warmer. Not a finer place on earth than Cornwall.'

'Viola!' Ellie took two long strides forward and took the small bale of straw out of the elderly woman's hands. 'You should've called. I would've brought the hay. Look. The little lad's up on all fours already. Have you decided what you going to call him?'

'Well,' the white-haired woman said, squinting against the midday sun. 'We're on an X year, so… Xavier? Xander?'

'X?' Lucas echoed. 'You've been raising alpacas for twenty-four years?'

Viola gave Lucas an appraising look. 'Not just a pretty face, are you?'

Lucas laughed. 'I spent some time at a clinic up north where we used to go to quite a few dairy farms.' He glanced at Ellie. They'd done the internship together. It had been the first time they'd lived together. A preview, he'd thought, of the life they would share together. From the pained look on her face she must've thought the same. He rubbed his hands together. 'Anyway, several of the farmers used the alphabet to track the birthing years.'

'X,' said Ellie, turning her attention to the cria, wobbling its way to its mum for a first drink. 'Um…how about Xanthus?'

Viola pressed her wrinkled hands to her heart. 'Xanthus?'

'What on earth made you think of that name?'

Ellie pointed up at the sky and playfully said, 'Divine inspiration?'

Viola's features softened. 'I was once courted by a young man called Xanthus.'

'Oh?' Ellie gave Lucas a *this-should-be-interesting* look.

'Yes.' Viola's gaze drifted out to the sea. 'He was a sailor. Naturally,' she added. 'With a name like that what else would he be?'

'A Greek god?' Lucas suggested.

'He was a touch of that, too,' Viola said, her look growing even more distant as the memories crowded in. 'He had blond hair. A bit like yours... Lucas, was it?'

Lucas smiled and nodded. Viola clearly didn't watch Uber-Vet either.

'Yes. We met when the motor on his fishing vessel gave out a few miles off the coast. One of the other boats saw his emergency signal and towed him and his crew in. He stayed at The Hungry Pelican.'

'Oh?' Ellie said, more interested.

'Long before your parents ran it, of course, Ellie, dear. It was a bit more...rustic, but, as pubs often are, it was the heart of the village, especially on a Saturday night.'

'And did you meet on a Saturday?'

'Friday,' she said wistfully, as if she'd never had a Friday since. 'Yes, we met on a Friday night and by Saturday night we were firmly in love. That's how it was done back in the day. None of these long courtships you young people seem to have.' She arched an eyebrow at Lucas as if she knew all about him.

Lucas shifted uncomfortably. He'd fallen in love with Ellie the moment he'd laid eyes on her. So why had he taken so damn long to propose? It wasn't as if he'd expected his love to run dry once vet school had finished. Putting family first had always seemed the right thing to do, but…he'd wanted a family with Ellie, too. Why had he made them two separate things?

'Three, four, ten years! I don't know what you young folk are waiting for,' Viola continued. 'Of course, with the war and rationing and heaven knows what else, none of us expected to live quite so long back then…'

Her eyes took on a faraway look as she reached out to an alpaca who had spotted the hay and come up to the fence line to have a munch.

As if she couldn't stop the story from being told, Viola continued. 'He asked me to go back with him. Xanthus. Leave Cornwall behind for Greece. Start our own family. I told him not to be ridiculous, we would stay here.'

Her lips pressed into a thin, pink line.

'And…?' prompted Ellie, throwing a *See, it isn't only me* look in Lucas's direction.

'And then his motor got fixed and I never heard from him again.' Viola gave Ellie a tight smile then lavished the alpaca mum with praise about how beautiful she was. How her love was pure. Unconditional.

That one stuck in Lucas's throat. He'd made his love for Ellie conditional. But what was he meant to have done? Left his family to flounder? Dragged Ellie into unknown levels of debt? The show had been a fluke. He'd thought he'd been protecting everyone. But… to what end?

'I'm so sorry,' Ellie said, her voice scratchy with emotion. Lucas looked over at her. She gave a shake of her head and looked away quickly, but he could've sworn he'd seen a film of tears in her eyes.

'Don't be, dear.' Viola gave her arm a squeeze, the sharp, savvy glint returning to her eyes. 'If I wasn't worth fighting for, then I'm sure it would've all turned out horribly anyway.'

Ellie suddenly became very busy packing up the rest of their equipment.

'I'm sure you were worth fighting for,' Lucas said, his eyes catching Ellie's as Viola batted his comment away. A flash of pain shot across her features so vividly it felt as though it had slashed through his own heart.

He ached to say, *I fought for you.* In his own way he had. By setting her free. Would she have really wanted to weather the storm with him? Put her dreams on hold to fulfil a family responsibility?

The thought sank deep into his gut. If she had…he would've been by her side as she'd carried their child. Their son.

Viola gave a wistful sigh. 'Look at you two. So young. So much life left to live Everything exciting that's happened to me happened before either of you were even born.'

Ellie squeaked in dismay. 'Oh, Viola. That's not true. Look at the difference you've made to the clinic. Without you, we wouldn't have the surgical wing.'

Viola waved the statement away.

Ellie persisted. 'You've got such a lovely farm and so many friends. Your family *adore* you.'

Viola gave them a look, dismayed at Ellie's naivety. 'They adore my money, love. Not me. I'd give it all away right now if I didn't have all of these lovely beasts to take care of.'

'I'm sure it's not the money.' Ellie's protest was weakening.

'No, dear. Much like me, my family like animals more than humans. The truth is, the likes of Caspian could do with rolling his sleeves up the way you do. Learn how to earn his keep.' She gave the alpaca another appraising look then spoke as if she were a High Court judge. 'I would strongly advise the two of you to seize the day. You never know what's round the corner. Or who you might lose when you turn it.' She brightened and gave each of them a quick head-to-toe inspection. 'You're both so tall the two of you. You'd make a fine couple. Ellie? What about keeping this one?'

Ellie flushed a deep red and muttered something about having another call to get to. Then, as if she'd been having a tug-of-war with her conscience about what the right thing to do was, she pulled Viola into a quick, fierce hug and said, 'You come down to the clinic anytime. You know we have the kettle on round the clock and there is always someone there to talk with.'

Viola gave her a smile and said she would definitely take her up on the offer.

After Ellie had headed back to the van and was safely out of earshot, Viola gave Lucas a schoolmarmish look and said, 'She won't wait for ever, you know.'

'Sorry?'

'Don't play the fool with me, my dear. I remember you.'

Lucas tried to remember when he might have crossed paths with Viola during one of his visits with Ellie back in the day. Truth was, he'd only had eyes for her, so apart from her parents and Drew he didn't really remember anyone else.

'*Carpe diem*, love,' Viola whispered. '*Carpe diem.*'

He knew what she was saying. This was his chance and he was already risking losing it.

'I'll see what I can do.'

'Yes,' said Viola pointedly. 'Do.'

Ellie slammed the van door shut, barely waiting for Lucas to close his door before reversing the vehicle out of the barnyard and onto the country lane.

She felt his eyes on her, but refused to look at him, finally exhaling when he sat back in a thoughtful silence.

She flicked on the radio and punched up an alternative music show. The singer was howling away about a following his dreams. It was the type of music her mother would've called shouting with instruments.

The perfect atmosphere for letting her own thoughts run wild.

What on earth had possessed Viola? *Keep this one.* She would've if she could've, but if there was one thing she'd learnt when Lucas Williams had handed her her walking papers? It was that no one had the power to make anyone stay.

Yup. That's right. She'd begged. The most humiliating thing she'd ever done. Begged and cried and asked over and over why he was doing this. He'd been immovable. Like a man whose heart had turned to stone.

When she'd gone home, Drew had been the one to tell her parents. She hadn't had the strength. The strength to say it without bawling her eyes out anyway and the last thing she wanted to do was shed a solitary tear for Lucas ever again. She'd vowed to never, ever let herself feel so low. So unworthy.

And, then, of course, she'd felt even lower when a couple of months later he'd popped up on telly with an utterly gorgeous woman on his arm. This, just about when she'd found out she was carrying their child.

'Can you be honest with me, Lucas?' The question was out before she could stop it. 'I need to know why you really came back. I know Henry rang you, but with your contacts you could've surely found someone else to fill in for us here these couple of months.'

Lucas turned in his seat and looked at

her. 'I think we both know I'm six years late, Ellie.'

'For what?' she pressed. 'Winning my love? Winning Maverick's? That took about five seconds. What is it you're really after, Lucas? Absolution? A clear conscience? It sure as hell isn't me.'

She saw Lucas give his knees a scrub then balled his hands into fists. Good. He was as frustrated as she was.

'Can we maybe have this talk somewhere stationary?'

'What?' She glared at him. 'Now my driving's not good enough for you either?' She swerved to miss a pothole, silently acquiescing that perhaps he had a point.

'Do we have any more calls to make?'

She threw him a guilty look. 'No. I just…' She stopped herself when her voice cracked then began again. 'I found Viola's story upsetting.'

'Not inspiring?'

She pulled the car off into a little recess in the hedge, twisted her leg round so she was facing him and said, 'Seriously? You think I would find a story about meeting the love of your life only to have him dump you at the first hurdle inspiring?'

'No.' Lucas reached out and swept some of her hair away from her face. 'I suppose not.'

'Lucas,' Ellie said, swiping his hand away. 'Why. Are. You. Here?'

He opened his mouth and closed it for a minute. Annoyingly, he looked completely adorable. All lost for words and clearly wanting to say the right thing but not knowing how. If this were seven years ago, she would've reached out, held his face in her hands, pulled him to her and kissed him.

But it wasn't then. It was now. Six years after he'd taken back his proposal. She had a child to look after. Her own heart to protect. And a veterinary clinic to run.

'Speak, man, or I am quite happy to find however many locums it takes to replace you and hand you your walking papers.'

'No.' Lucas shook his head solidly, the passion in his voice matching hers. 'Not now that I've met Mav.'

A chill ran down Ellie's spine. 'You are not taking him from me.'

'No.' Lucas said. 'But I— Can we walk and talk?'

She nodded. 'There's a footpath down here.'

He gave the thick hedge she'd parked the van alongside a dubious look.

'There's a way through to a lovely little river. I bring Esmerelda down here sometimes with Mav.'

'It's not where you bring people to disappear them?'

'It's where I go for picnics,' she said dryly as she got out of the car and grabbed her backpack from behind her seat. 'C'mon. I've got sandwiches. You want to walk and talk? Follow me.'

They set off at a brisk pace under the cool canopy of trees, Ellie doing her best to stay a step ahead of Lucas. Every emotion under the sun was zipping through her bloodstream right now, but the number one thing she didn't want to do was cry. Neither did she want to shout about her son's future. He was hers. Yes, Lucas had a right to have access to him. It was only fair to Mav, but…she'd go down fighting if Lucas suddenly slapped a custody agreement in front of her.

All of which threw her hackles and her suspicions straight back up into the stratosphere. She wheeled on him. 'Are you sure you didn't know about Maverick before you came down?'

'Absolutely. Henry didn't say a word. He just said you were in a pickle because of Drew's accident.'

'A pickle?' Ellie laughed. 'He called nearly losing my best friend and business partner to a car accident a pickle?'

'Henry was always the master of under-statement.'

She threw up her hands. 'Looks like there's yet another person I didn't know as well as I thought I did.' She tipped her head up to the sky and squeezed her eyes shut tight. No. She was not this person. She was not an embittered, angry person. She'd worked so hard to put the past in the past. This was a hiccough. An emotionally charged, life-changing hiccough. She looked at Lucas determined not to let her emotions get the better of her. Stomping away in a huff did not pay dividends. 'What else did he say?' Ellie pointed Lucas towards the path that led to the river, a little too aware of their arms brushing each time the higgledy-piggledy path brought them closer together.

'He said you had an amazing facility. That I should take inspiration from you.'

'What? You've got all of the bells and whistles at your disposal in London.'

'Not any more.'

'What?'

Lucas wiped his hands together. 'That chapter in my life is done and dusted.'

'Right. At the ripe age of thirty-five you've finished with Uber-Vet for ever. What happens when you realise that you miss the celeb lifestyle and change your mind, beg them to take you back?'

'Seriously, Ells—Ellie.' He corrected with one of those goofy *oops* smiles of his. 'Henry's taken over the show permanently.'

It still wasn't an answer.

'Lucas!' She stomped her foot. 'Will you please tell me why, of all the veterinary clinics in the world, you had to come help out at mine?'

'Because I needed you to know how awful I felt about what had happened. Make peace with you. Can we do that? Try to make things right between us?'

Ellie stared at him solidly, her expression still, then after what felt like ages she said, 'You should know by now not to say things you don't mean.'

Lucas meant it. That had always been his intention in coming down here. What had shocked him were the words he hadn't said. *I still love you.*

They reverberated around his heart as if the words had been inscribed there.

He looked deep into Ellie's eyes, wondering

if she was feeling the same thing. A long-lost feeling that could be revitalised. Renewed.

I still love you.

The words gained traction as his heart pounded the words out in a syncopated cadence.

I still love you.

He couldn't say them. Not yet anyway.

Viola's words rang in his head. *Carpe diem.* Fine. He'd do something about it. But step by step. No way was he going to scare her away. Not with a relationship with his son on the line. 'I mean it, Ells.' Lucas pressed his fists to his heart. 'Just because things turned out the way they did, it never meant I stopped caring about you. Splitting up hurt me every bit as much—'

'Oh, hold on a minute, Lucas. Splitting up with me served you and you only, so let's ratchet back the sanctimonious *I was doing this for both of us* attitude, shall we?' Ellie distractedly pulled her hair up into a top knot, then tugged it down, then tangled it up again until finally leaving it to its own devices as she sat down on a tree stump by the edge of the river.

Okay. Fair enough. But she was still here. Still listening.

Lucas sat next to her, channelling his energies into digging deep into his soul to find the best solution. He loved her. Now he needed to find out what the hell to do with it. Stuff it back in the box where he'd put it all those years ago? Or rebuild the trust he'd so obviously broken by taking matters into his own hands.

Tension buzzed between them like high-tensile electricity.

'I— There were many things I wish I'd done better.'

She shot him a sharp wounded look.

'I know, I know. It's a cheap way of explaining myself, but…' He tried to lay out the facts so she could understand. 'After I proposed, I called my family to tell them the good news.'

A wary look shadowed her eyes.

'It turned out things at home were very complicated. Nothing to do with you. They all love you and think you're brilliant, but… they'd been waiting until I finished vet school to tell me just how bad things were.'

Her shoulders dropped a notch. 'What happened?'

'Jonty went AWOL, for one.'

'What? He just disappeared?'

'Pretty much.'

'But I thought he was meant to take over

your father's practice so you could come to Cornwall?'

Lucas gave her a wry smile. Families. They were complicated. And Lucas's was no different.

'Turns out, as the deadline approached, Jonty's drinking increased. So had his time at the races.'

Ellie raised her eyebrows. She knew too much champagne and access to horseracing wasn't a good combo for Jonty. It was one of the reasons it had been agreed Jonty would work with his father. So he could be reined in, so to speak.

'Long story short,' Lucas continued, 'a lifetime of trying to become the man our father wanted Jonty to be landed him in rehab. The clinic hadn't been doing well the more Dad's Parkinson's progressed, but he'd been too damn proud to tell anyone until Jonty upped and left and I called to tell him I was moving to Cornwall.'

'But didn't he know? We'd talked about it for ages.'

'Course he did. I guess he'd just been hoping Jonty's wild phase would come to an end, but it was one of those awful convergences of bad timing, bad debt and poor health. It was going to take an epic amount of energy to turn things round at my dad's clinic. Years. I didn't know what else to do. There was no way I was going to drag you down with me. Believe me, I genuinely thought I was doing the right thing.'

A wash of compassion softened Ellie's features as she inspected the new landscape of her memories. For the first time since he'd come down he felt a glimmer of hope that they could be like they had once been. Best friends, confidants, lovers. They'd known everything about each other. He'd thought they always would. And then life had intervened.

'Lucas…' Ellie's voice was cautious, as if she wasn't sure she wanted to go down this road but was going to make herself, if only to find peace. 'One of the things I always admired about you was your sense of honour. It was why it shook me to the core when you split up with me.'

'I did what I did because I believed it was honourable. If there had been any other way…' He brushed a bit of her hair behind her ear then ran his finger down her sweet face again. 'It was such an incredibly complicated, unhappy time for my family.'

'So…' Her eyes connected with his with a primeval intensity. As if she could actually see directly into his heart. 'In your weird, backwards way you were protecting me by breaking things off?'

He nodded. That had been exactly it.

The softness in her features hardened again. 'You should've trusted me to stand by you.'

He snorted. 'What? Burden you with debt and put years between you and the dream of opening the Dolphin Cove Clinic? No way. I would never have done that. Not to you or Drew.'

'Drew would've understood.'

He gave his jaw a scrub. Yeah. Drew probably would have. He'd not even bothered asking. It had just seemed too much to ask of a friend.

Ellie poked his thigh. 'And I'd just promised to marry you. To stick with you. Through everything.'

Lucas felt his ribcage expand and contract. The emotional weight of all he'd put her through hit him like a wrecking ball. Little wonder she'd kept Maverick a secret. He didn't know if he would've trusted him to come through for her either. Not after what he'd put her through.

'Do you think there's a chance we could start over? As friends...for Mav?'

She blew out a slow breath. 'I don't know,

Lucas. I'm not sure I can go back to the way things were.'

'I disagree.' He softened his tone. 'I know it'll take work. I know it'll take time. But I believe we can fix this, Ellie. What we had was…it was out of this world. And something's telling me you feel it, too.'

She lifted her hands up. 'Whoa, there, sonny boy. Having you here is a reminder of the one time in my entire life when I felt small, insignificant. You made me feel worthless and I promised myself I would never, ever feel that way again.'

'I don't want you to feel that way again.' He meant it with every fibre of his being.

'I know,' she said. 'Maybe. There are six years of resenting you for not believing in me that I need to sort out.' She lifted up a hand so she could explain herself. 'Look. I don't want to be angry at you. I don't want to hate you. I don't want to resent you. I want Maverick to have a dad.' Her serious expression lit up with a gentle smile. 'And even though you're pretty new at it, you seem to be catching onto this whole dad thing pretty well.'

Lucas knew now was not the time to accept kudos. He nodded for her to continue.

'Now that I understand why you did what you did a bit more, I can let a lot of that pent-up *grr* out.' She made another *grr* and feigned watching it disappear down the lane.

'It's a big ask.' Obviously. 'Asking you to forgive me.'

'I want to forgive you. I… I do.' She gave him a look he couldn't read. 'You know what my mum says about things like this.'

He nodded, smiling as she threw some air quotes up and said, 'There's no point carrying around anger or defensiveness when gravity is already against you.' She picked up a stick and began to trace a swirl into the earth. 'Rotten things happen. Quite a few epically rotten things happened to you. But you should've believed that as your fiancée, as your *wife*, I would've wanted nothing more than to be there, by your side, supporting you, loving you. For that alone I… I'm going to struggle, Lucas. I will try to be friends. Honestly, I will, but…sorry. Forgiveness isn't going to come easily to me.' When she met his eyes, he saw all he needed to know. She still loved him. And that's why the hurt ran so deep.

He wanted to push it. Press her to admit she felt that same heated frisson whenever their hands brushed. Notice how charged the atmosphere between them was when their eyes met and the space between them took on a magnetic quality. They were meant for one another. Always had been. He knew it in his marrow. She did too. But she was protecting herself. She was being cautious.

'Friends?' he said, extending a hand.

Friends,' she repeated sadly.

The moment her hand touched his… With work and commitment, one day, somehow, everything would be all right again, and they could finally be a family.

CHAPTER SIX

'LUC!' ELLIE KNOCKED on the guest flat door. 'You in there?'

No answer.

She glanced out at the bay beyond the flat's balcony. The summer sun was just dipping below the horizon, the sea sparkling like diamonds. A perfect night for a romantic stroll...

Er... No, it wasn't. It was a perfect night to perform surgery on a Labrador retriever who could very likely die if someone didn't answer his blinking door soon!

'Lucas?' She tried again, tapping her foot impatiently. Maybe he was out. *Urgh.* Not tonight! She needed him. She glanced at her watch then out at the clinic car park. They'd be arriving any minute now.

She blinked back some frustrated tears. She wasn't sad. Or mad. She was tired, mostly. The last few months of trying to run everything with Drew in hospital had been wearing. Just having him back in Dolphin Cove eased her stress. Saying that, with the amount of rehab he was still facing? The truth of the matter was Drew was still several weeks away from consulting let alone operating. A hard-hitting reminder that the clinic ran much better with two vets and even more smoothly with three.

She knocked again. *C'mon, c'mon, c'mon! Answer the bloody door!*

Maybe he'd gone into the village to visit Drew. When he could prise him out of the house, that was. Drew had definitely become a bit of a hermit. She reeled back through the evening. Nope. Not likely. She'd been down at the Pelican an hour ago to give Mav a goodnight kiss before he went upstairs for Grandma and Grandpa night, a summertime special. She'd not seen Lucas or Drew and Drew would have definitely pulled her aside for an update on the 'Lucas situation'.

Meaning had she decided to fall in love with him again? Drew thought she would. Ellie insisted she wouldn't. Out loud anyway. They'd achieved a perfectly civilised working relationship and she made sure not to be too protective when it came to the time he wanted to spend with Mav. Ignoring the way her heart pounded when she saw the two of them together or the way her body responded whenever his hands brushed against hers was rather tricky but…she was made of stern stuff. She had to stay strong. Resistant to the Lucas Effect.

She banged on the door again. 'Lucas!' She was going to have to do this on her own if he didn't answer in thirty seconds.

She racked her mind. Where could he be? Apart from the pub and a couple of small restaurants, there wasn't really anywhere else to go in Dolphin Cove. Not at this hour anyway. He'd said something about running some errands for Drew a couple of days back. But errands at nine o'clock at night?

Her heart lurched up into her throat.

He wouldn't…no, he wouldn't be out on a date, would he? Not that she cared. He could do what he liked with his life as long as he didn't hurt Mav.

She pictured him laughing with another woman and reaching out to hold her hand.

A swirl of nausea rose in her throat.

She did care.

Well, not tonight she didn't. Tonight she was a vet and vets didn't have time to be all jealous over imaginary dates their ex-fiancé may or may not be on. She knocked one final time. 'Lucas!'

The door swung open and all the silly thoughts that had been swirling round her head disappeared when there, lit by the remaining glow of the evening's sun, was Lucas Williams with nothing but a towel round his waist.

Oh, *my*. She didn't know how, but she'd forgotten how completely and totally gorgeous he was when he wasn't wearing clothes. In fact, he was even more scrumptious if that was at all possible. The golden remains of the day lit him to perfection. Damp hair tumbling in soft waves on his forehead. Little droplets of water shifting their way slowly across his musculature. And then, to her horror, she licked her lips.

She must've looked like the cat who'd got the cream.

He gave her a funny look, then gestured for her to look up from his six-pack to his eyes.

She put on a cranky managerial face and barked, 'Where've you been?'

Why are you speaking like a possessive girlfriend?

'Out for a run. Everything okay?' He looked over her shoulder towards her flat, presumably to check for Mav.

His question snapped her back to the reason why she'd knocked.

'We've got an emergency gastro surgery I need help with.'

Everything about him snapped from relaxed to action man. 'Absolutely. Let me get some clothes on.'

She was about to say *No, don't* because it was exactly the kind of thing she would've said back in the day, but that would've been flirting and maybe sexist and completely because she wanted to keep staring at his utterly luscious torso. It was broad and tanned and screaming to be traced by the tips of her fingers. To her horror, she actually physically ached to be one of the drops of water casually working its way down his pecs all the way to his six-pack. A light strip of blond hair naughtily beckoned to her...wending its way from just below his belly button to the edges of his loosely wrapped towel. The sun flared inside each of the glistening droplets of water dappled along his shoulders, his chest, his mouth. Droplets of water she would envy until the end of time because of that stupid, stupid vow she'd made him take that they would only be friends.

No. Not stupid. Practical.

And she'd done extremely well in compartmentalising everything to get work done, address the fact her son now knew his father and that, more to the point, she absolutely, positively did not and would not ever fall for Lucas Williams ever again.

The pickle was...now that it was mid-August and Lucas only had a few weeks left...it suddenly didn't seem enough. He filled a hole in her life she'd not wanted to admit needed filling. Drew was brilliant and her bestie, but Lucas? Lucas knew what she was going to say before she said it. Could tell which puppy she loved most without her having to say. Knew when she needed a hug and some quiet time after putting down a family's cherished pet. Predicted when she could do with a completely silly three-legged race with her son along the beach with the promise of ice-cream cones at the end. She hated to admit it, but the last three weeks of 'friendship' had been fun.

Oh, who was she kidding? It had been more than that.

It had been a glimpse into the family they might have been if life had been different. The more she'd hashed over the talk she'd had with Lucas, the more she could see why he'd made the decisions he had. Did she agree with them? No. He'd left her with a broken heart and a son to raise on her own, but if her parents' pub had been put in peril and there was no chance she could've done the clinic with Lucas…

How did you choose?

You didn't.

You went with your gut and on that occasion? Family had won. She got it. Her family had been her bedrock throughout her life. Even more so when she'd found herself alone, pregnant, and with nothing more than a dream of opening a veterinary clinic.

Her parents had been pretty awesome this summer, too. Taking Lucas's arrival in their stride. Never mind the fact her mum had been gently prodding at her for years to tell him. But she didn't rub it in. Say, *See? Look how happy your son is with his father.* They simply made Lucas welcome at the occasional 'family' meal down at the pub and never raised a questioning eyebrow when, on the very rare occasion Ellie loosened her mama bear reins, Lucas came to pick up Mav instead of her. Her parents were, in short, the completely reliable, loving, amazing people they'd always been and, perhaps like her, were waiting to see if Lucas really was here to make amends.

'Ells? Is this surgery happening now?'

'Yes,' she said, distractedly flicking her fingers at his torso. 'Go put some clothes on and I'll see you in the clinic.'

'What's it for?'

'Chocolate Lab who ate an entire bucket of lead fishing weights.'

Lucas let out a low whistle. 'Hell's teeth. Shown any signs of poisoning?'

'Nope. Just clanking.'

His eyes widened. 'Clanking?'

'He ate that many.' She mimed being a Lab with a low hanging stomach that clanked.

Lucas rolled his eyes in disbelief. 'What sort of Dolphin Cove family would let their dog eat a bucket of lead fishing weights?'

Ellie smiled. She'd never admit it, but she loved how he'd taken to speaking about Dolphin Cove as if he were a local. He knew as well as she did that even if he lived here fifty years, they'd still think of him as a Londoner.

'They aren't local.' Ellie gestured towards the main road. 'It's a family visiting from London. They were playing down on the beach, building a sandcastle or something with their little ones, and lost track of the dog who they found wolfing down the last one. There were bits of crab in there, apparently.'

'Ah. Lab, you say?'

'Yup.'

'Chocolate?'

'Mmm-hmm.'

'They're the hungriest, by my estimation.'

'Pretty much.'

Lucas looked over her shoulder. 'Where's Mav? What's our plan for him?'

Ellie's heart unexpectedly bashed against her chest. Lucas's question had come so organically it felt as if they were a proper family. Sometimes she brought a sleep monitor down with her. Other times she called Drew. Today timing was on their side. 'He's at my parents' tonight. It's board games night at the pub, remember? He usually stays over, so... lucky for the Lab owners you and I have a completely free twelve hours ahead of us. It's you and me, baby.'

She made a face.

You and me, baby? What the hell was that? She readjusted her features to make it look as if she'd said nothing more interesting than *I'll prepare the surgical tray.*

When she met Lucas's blue eyes, something passed through them she couldn't quite put a finger on. A tangle of emotions. Relief that Maverick was being looked after? Something...naughty? Or maybe he was just looking forward to a good juicy surgery. That had to be it. He wouldn't be thinking sexy thoughts at a time like this. With a dog's life in peril.

'See you down there in two minutes,'

Lucas said, turning around, door still open, and with a dramatic flourish…he whipped off his towel.

The cheeky bastard.

She stared at his bum and couldn't help but smile. Toned, saucy—if that was any way to describe sexy bum cheeks—and just begging to be squeezed.

He turned back to make sure she was looking.

Oh, she was looking all right.

With a wink and a grin, he was gone.

It was going to be a *long* night.

'Could I have those surgical scissors again, please?'

Lucas was a picture of concentration.

Ellie handed him the specialist scissors. 'Gastronomic incision not big enough?'

'Not…just…yet…' Lucas's brow crinkled. '*Boom*. Now it is. I'll just pop a suture in at either end to bring it closer to the abdominal incision…'

His voice tapered off as he meticulously went through the steps of preparing the chocolate Lab for surgery.

'Antibiotics all right?' Ellie was in full surgical mode now. The poor dog had literally clanked on his weighted walk into the clinic and the longer that lead was inside him, the more likely a case of internal lead poisoning could threaten his life.

'Twenty milligrams for every sixty minutes.' Lucas glanced at the operating theatre's digital clock. 'We've been at it for twenty minutes. Another forty and we'll give him a second injection, unless we've got it wrapped up by then.'

'Right. Let's get going.'

Ellie and Lucas went about the surgery as if no time at all had passed since they'd last been in a surgery together. Surprisingly, this was the first they'd done together since he'd arrived. She suggested he take the lead—not because she wasn't up to it. Adrenaline always kicked her skill levels to the fore whenever an emergency case landed at the clinic. It was more…she really liked watching him work. He had an incredibly exacting but relaxed way of preparing an animal for surgery. Not clinical like some of the locums she'd worked with. It was almost like watching a conductor at work. He always made sure the dog knew he was there, keeping him safe with soft strokes and the odd little massage on his head as he drifted off to sleep when the anaesthetic kicked in.

They worked together in studied silence for

a while, only breaking the atmosphere with a request for a pair of clamps or laparotomy sponges to keep the intestinal loop isolated from the rest of the abdominal cavity.

'Strewth,' said Lucas as he pulled out another lead weight. 'Looks like there are four more to go. There must be almost a kilo's worth of them. Poor pooch.'

'I know, right?' Ellie took the weight and put it in a bag marked for post-operative disposal. 'Lord Fluffingstein may never eat crabs again.'

'I doubt that.' Lucas sniggered. 'A Lab's a Lab no matter what they've been through.' He asked Ellie to secure a clamp to help elevate the stomach. As she worked, he laughed. 'I've come across some cracking dog names before, but his takes the cake. Lord Fluffingstein. What do you think they call him when he's running around at the park?'

'Your Lordship?' Ellie ventured.

Lucas gave a snort, his twinkling eyes and jiggling eyebrows the only things visible above his surgical mask. He put on a fancy voice and intoned, 'Your Lordship would like to offer his utmost gratitude to Her Ladyship Ellie van Stonington for having the very best of clinics to hand at his time of need.'

Mercifully, Lucas couldn't see the flush of

red creeping up her neck. Thank goodness for surgical gowns!

'Would Her Ladyship be so kind as to give the saline bag a bit of squeeze, please?' He looked across the operating table, hands poised to retrieve the next weight, and winked.

Gah!

How was it a gastro-intestinal surgery on a greedy chocolate Labrador had turned into a flirtation zone?

No veterinarian brain surgeons necessary to answer that one.

The Lucas Williams Effect had permeated her very finely crafted no-flirtation shield. Naked bums did that to a girl. His anyway.

The long night was turning into a dangerous one. For her erogenous zones anyway. She cleared her thoughts and put on her grown-up voice to veer him off course. 'It could've been a fatal night for him. I know the Penzance clinic has had at least two dogs die this summer from lead poisoning.'

'Sounds like there's a need for some signs to be posted down at the harbour or a bit more diligence by the fishermen.'

'I think the dog owners should be the responsible parties, really. It's not like you'd let your children wander off and stick their heads into a bucket of mystery food.'

'Good point.' Lucas said. 'Although… I seem to remember seeing a picture of Maverick with a face full of spaghetti Bolognese sauce down at the pub.'

Ellie barked a laugh. 'My mum's spaghetti Bolognese is worth a face-dive. And I was obviously there to observe the occasion, as every good parent is.' She eased another laparotomy sponge into place then looked up to catch the tail end of Lucas's wince.

'Sorry. That wasn't meant to be a jibe.'

'No offence taken.' He didn't sound angry. Wistful maybe. Definitely more pensive than he'd just been.

She couldn't even imagine having missed so much of Maverick's life. It had taken all her strength to stop herself from nipping over to the school in her breaks when he'd first started last year. This year would most likely be no different. Even on his nights at her parents' she demanded a full retelling of the evening. Lucas had missed five entire years of his son's life.

For the first time she felt a huge rush of empathy for all the years he'd lost because she'd decided her son would be better off without him. Oh, crumbs. Had her decision-making been as messed up as Lucas's had been? Had she kept Maverick out of his life out of spite? Hurt, definitely. She had to admit to that. She'd told herself over and over that someone who broke such huge promises wouldn't be reliable. She glanced across at him, his attention back on the extraction of yet another lead weight. She'd wanted him to trust her in his darkest moment and then she'd gone and done the exact same thing to him. She'd shut him out. Shut him out when she'd needed him most.

Oh, Lucas. I'm so sorry.

As tangled up as her emotions were about having Lucas here, she knew one thing for certain. They would have to make this work for Maverick's sake. He already adored Lucas and it was easy to see Lucas felt exactly the same way. Not that she blamed him. Her kid was one in a billion.

She adopted a chirpier tone. 'My parents are on the village council. I'll see if they can mention it. Even if the signs are posted in the summer when all of the tourists are here.'

'Nice one. Oh, and can you remind me to send Lord Fluffingstein home with a list of things to watch out for just in case some of the lead did get into his system? And about peritonitis.'

'I already did it. The lead part.'

'They didn't stick around?' His eyebrows rose in surprise.

'I told them I'd ring when we were done. Their children looked knackered and teary. Their holiday cottage is only a five-minute walk away, so I thought a few text updates would be better than them fretting it out in Reception.

Lucas eased another weight out of the dog's intestinal tract and considered it for a moment. 'What's this?'

Ellie leant in, a hint of Lucas's citrusy shower gel hitting her along with another mental image of his cheeky *derrière* sashaying out of the lounge and into his bedroom.

'Someone's initials most likely,' she squeaked.

'The fisherman's?'

'Probably. If they're hand cast like these ones obviously were, they sometimes stamp their IDs into the mould. Must be an old-timer.'

'Smart.'

'Not if you don't want someone taking your crab it isn't. Cornish common sense. The traps will be marked, the buoys, everything. My dad told me the medieval fisherman would use little symbols if they were illiterate. It's a shame really because in theory it should be done on the honour system.

Everyone knowing where everyone's patch is and steering clear. Respect and consideration and honesty. That's all the world needs to work properly, isn't it?'

'Is that a variation on love making the world go round?'

Her eyes shot to his. 'I suppose. But love *is* respect and honesty. In an ideal world,' she tacked on, not wanting this to sound like a lecture.

'A village that fishes together stays together?' He suggested.

'Yes! Exactly.'

Crinkles fanned out at Lucas's blue eyes as he handed her yet another weight. He was smiling. A ridiculously large flock of butterflies took flight in her tummy. Mercy. The Lucas Williams Effect. Right here in her OR. She forced herself to become more officious.

'Still an idealist, then, I see,' he said.

'Still a dreamer,' she parried.

'Exactly what I always loved about you,' he said. 'Aiming high and refusing to settle for second best.'

What he'd loved *about her?*

The minute the words came out of Lucas's mouth he knew he'd stepped onto emotional quicksand.

Ellie's eyes flared brightly and then grew distant.

If kicking himself had been an option, he'd be covering himself in bruises.

How the hell had he let that nugget of truth slip out?

Because it *was* the truth. He loved her. Plain and simple. Seeing her again had had exactly the same lightning-strike effect it had had the first time he'd seen her. He loved her and he didn't want to hold the feelings captive any more. But he had to. His feelings on marriage...they were complicated. So much more tangled than being here in Dolphin Cove, with Ellie, with Maverick...

It felt like living again. Living his own life away from the camera, away from his family's intense reliance on him to get them out of a very deep hole. *Breathing* felt more real. He'd quite happily never go back to London again if she would have him here, but another part of him was worried it was all just a bubble. A bubble that would burst just as it had all those years ago when he'd proposed and thought absolutely nothing could break through the intense joy he'd felt.

Despite the dark thoughts, he smiled beneath his surgical mask. The *look* on Ellie's face when he'd whipped off his towel. The attraction they'd once had was there all right. She still fancied him. He definitely fancied her. Could she love him again? Love *and* trust him the way she once had? Could he trust her? She had, after all, kept his son a secret. If he hadn't come down here, would he have ever known he had a son?

They worked in silence for a bit, teasing away the foreign bodies, ensuring the beloved pet was as well cared for as if he were one of their own. It had been their shared motto back in the day. 'Treat them as you'd treat your own.'

He silently cursed himself. He'd treated Ellie incredibly poorly. Turned his back on her precisely when he should've held his arms out wide open and said, *I need you.* Somewhere deep inside him he knew she still had feelings for him. He saw it in her eyes. Not all the time, but…it was there. A core-deep need to earn that trust back gripped him. He wanted his son in his life—no question. But he also wanted Ellie in it. How that relationship took form? He didn't know. But he knew shared trust would be of paramount importance. If it took him the rest of his life to earn back her trust, so be it.

'Here's the last weight,' he said, his voice rough with emotion.

'You all right, Luc?'

Ellie's eyes met his, her forehead crinkled with concern.

She cared. More than she was willing to admit, but she cared.

That flame in his heart burnt a little bit brighter.

He nodded. 'We need to lavage the peritoneal cavity with some warm saline to remove any spillage or blood clots.'

She nodded, the furrows in her brow deepening. He was stating the obvious to avoid saying the words he wanted to say most.

I love you, Ellie.

He used a good two and a half litres of the sterile liquid to clean the area then checked the dog's vitals whilst Ellie used a surgical suction tube to remove the fluid and dry the cavity as much as possible. Hygiene was critical. An iota of infection and the poor pooch risked another visit to the clinic. One he might not return home from. When she'd finished and stepped back from the table, they both changed their gloves and then the instruments. When they'd finished Lucas asked. 'Want to close, or shall I?'

Ellie gave her forehead a swipe with the sleeve of her surgical gown. She looked tired. Really tired.

He couldn't believe he hadn't seen it before, but it was obvious wasn't it? The poor woman had been working herself to the bone since Drew's accident. He made a mental note to up his game on clinic hours. Call in some favours. Get her the time off she needed. Be here for her when she needed him. Properly.

Ellie placed fresh surgical towels around the edges of the laparotomy. 'I'm happy to close. I'm going to use a straightforward continuous suture pattern, so…if you need to get to bed or anything…' Her voice sounded smaller than it had. Less confident.

'No chance. I'm going to see this through with you.'

Her eyes flicked up to meet his. 'Okay. Can you text the family to let them know he'll be out of surgery in half an hour or so? He won't be up to much of a family cuddle, but I'm sure he'd love to hear their voices before we get him snugged down in the kennel overnight.'

'Will you send him home with them tomorrow?'

'Yup. Normally, I'd do it tonight, but it's so late and I'd like to triple-check there aren't any signs of lead poisoning tomorrow.'

Lucas sent the text then fielded the inevitable phone call, assuring the family that Lord Fluffingstein had come through surgery well.

Lucas said he'd meet them in the front of the clinic in half an hour, but not before as he was helping Ellie with the final stages of surgery. He watched as Ellie began to weave the synthetic absorbable monofilament sutures into Lord Fluffingstein's stomach. 'Nice,' he said. 'Perfect apposition of the gastrointestinal tract. I always remember you being a dab hand with a needle.'

Her eyes narrowed a bit. Whether she was smiling or shooting him a look, was difficult to tell. Lucas's stomach screwed up into a tight knot. Back in the day he would've been certain it was a smile.

'I've got some socks you could do for me in the morning,' he teased.

He grinned at the inevitable arched eyebrow she was sending him and began to hum.

'What's that?' she asked, tying off the final knot and pronouncing the surgery over. 'Sounds familiar.'

'"Hound Dog",' he said.

Ellie laughed. 'Of course it is! I can't believe I didn't recognise it straight away.'

He began to sing some of the lyrics, enjoying the sound of her laugh, the way her eyes lit up when they met his as she joined in on the chorus.

'Do you remember when you first sang it?'

she asked, her voice suddenly thick with nostalgia.

'Course.' He triple-checked that all of the tubes and needles were clear of Lord Fluffingstein before he and Ellie carefully transferred the pooch to a gurney so they could take him to the recovery kennels. 'Karaoke night the first week we met.'

'First night we kissed,' she added, her eyes meeting his as they wheeled the gurney down the short corridor to the recovery kennels, where a chihuahua with a torn cruciate ligament, a tom cat who'd met the wrong end of a barbed-wire fence and a geriatric cocker spaniel who'd had two hip replacements were already sleeping.

Together they slipped him into the kennel, his sleeping form heavy in their arms. There was something so vulnerable about a post-operative animal. 'It makes you feel so responsible, doesn't it? For their welfare.' His voice sounded loud in the quiet room. He lowered it. 'Seeing them so defenceless.'

'I feel that way when Mav's asleep, too.' Ellie shifted her body so that her arm brushed against his.

'I'm not surprised. I've only been with him a couple of times when he's been asleep, but...' He gave his chest a light thump. 'It gets you right here.' He remembered the weight of his sleeping son in his arms when he'd carried him to bed a few evenings back after a particularly long story-reading session at his place. He'd never felt anything more perfect. Never felt a stronger need to care for someone. It was unlike anything he'd ever experienced.

He put his hand on Lord Fluffingstein's soft ear and gave it a gentle caress. 'You just want to make sure they never hurt again. That they're always safe. Don't we, Lord Fluffingstein? We never ever want you to have to go through anything like this again.'

Ellie smiled at him, leaning against his shoulder for a split second. 'I knew you were still in there.'

'What? Who?'

'The big old softie I met all those years ago.'

'He was always in there. He just got a little lost along the way.' Their eyes met and clashed. He hoped his were telling her he was trying to change. Trying to be the man she'd once thought he was.

Her eyes stayed glued to his, a wash of understanding softening her features. 'Life can do that sometimes. Send you down a path you never expected to be on.'

It wasn't an outright 'I forgive you'…but it was close.

A huge warmth filled his chest as the space between them grew smaller, and smaller yet, until the next thing Lucas knew he was holding Ellie's face in his hands, tipping her chin up to his, their lips millimetres apart, then brushing, sparks of heat flaring between them until he couldn't bear the distance between them any longer.

He slid one hand into the small of her back and the other onto the nape of her neck, moulded her soft, curvaceous body to his until they were kissing as their lives depended upon it. Not urgently. More…as if every microsecond of contact mattered. Touching and teasing and parting and tasting. It felt familiar and completely new, as if time had granted them a reprieve from their past and given them this fresh start to see if maybe, just maybe, they could find a way to be together again.

And then the buzzer for the front door went.

Ellie pushed back, her hands on his chest, her eyes glued to his. 'We'd better get that.'

'When they're gone, I want to do this again.'

Ellie said nothing, but her body language told him all he needed to know. She did, too.

'You'd better go get the door.'

'No,' he said solidly. 'I think you should.'

'What? Have you gone all shy?'

He pointed at his scrubs.

Ellie's eyes dipped below his waistline and began to blink rapidly.

'Ah. Oh. Um… I'll just get the door, then, and give you a chance to…' She turned to go.

'Ellie?' He reached out and took her hand. She didn't try to pull it away.

'What?'

'I'm here for you, you know. Whatever you need.'

The flush of her cheeks told him she knew he was offering more than a helping hand in the OR. She gave his hand a quick, tight squeeze. 'Thank you. Now let's let give this family the good news, yeah?'

'Course.' He went to the sink and began to throw cold water on his face and the back of his neck. Once things had subsided down there…he looked in the mirror. Was he the same guy she'd once known? Yes. Was he different as well? Yes.

Older, wiser, hopefully better equipped to handle life's slings and arrows with a bit more perspective than he'd had back then, a twenty-nine-year-old man fresh out of ten years of training to be a vet. As he stared into the mirror, willing it to tell him what he was capable of, he felt a shift in his heart. He could do this. He could stay. Learn to trust himself enough to take another risk. Take his time earning Ellie's trust…and love. And no amount of cold water on his face would put out that fire. Not by a long shot.

CHAPTER SEVEN

ELLIE WAS NODDING and smiling and really wishing Lord Fluffingstein's family would go home and go to sleep because one too many carnal thoughts were getting in the way of her thinking sensibly.

She wanted Lucas.

Badly.

She wanted to run her fingers through his hair. She wanted to trace her fingers along that gorgeous chest and abdomen of his. She wanted to explore what had been happening in his scrubs before that ruddy buzzer had gone off, reminding her she was living in the here and now and not ten years ago when she and Lucas used to sneak off and take a post-operative shower together.

Her attention swung to the corridor where Lucas was taking long-legged strides to join them. And here was the reason why her mind couldn't stay focussed.

He slipped into place beside her, one of his big lovely warm hands on the small of her back as he extended the other. 'Hello, there. I'm Lucas Williams.'

The family went wide-eyed. 'You're the Uber-Vet,' whispered one of the children.

'Not any more,' Lucas said, his smile not faltering for a second. In fact, if Ellie wasn't mistaken, it had just grown brighter. He stood back up and put his hand back on Ellie's back, as if giving her a physical cue that he had really meant it when he'd said he was here for her.

Here for ever?

No.

She batted the thought away.

That would be ridiculous.

She looked up at him.

His eyes met hers and he dropped her a slow, astonishingly cheeky wink.

Oh, my God. He wanted to take a shower with her, too.

'The best thing you all can do for Lord Fluffingstein is to get yourselves a good night's sleep. He'll be needing lots of TLC in the morning.'

If Ellie wasn't mistaken, the pressure on her back had turned into a soft, circular rub at the mention of TLC.

Sprays of glittery anticipation made standing still incredibly awkward.

She was going to have sex. With her gorgeous ex. The father of her child no less. The first time she'd had sex in just about for ever. She'd had a couple of relationships over the years, but...*meh*. None of them had been Lucas and she had a business to run and a child to raise. His child.

'So we'll see you in the morning, then?' Lucas was shaking hands with the owners, then he knelt down to give the children a hug. No wonder he was famous and everyone who'd ever watched television was in love with him.

She was in— Wait, *was* she still in love him?

She watched the family go in a stunned silence.

No. She couldn't be...could she?

Lucas held out a hand, guiding her towards the back exit that led to their flat—her flat. Her flat at her clinic in her county—

'Shower, Ells?

'Yes,' she answered way too quickly and hilariously primly for someone filled to the brim with lust that surely could be sated on this one occasion. Once they'd had tonight she could get on with her life and be quite content. 'That would be lovely.'

'Mmm…' Lucas rolled over in bed, feeling the sun on his face. He patted his hand out alongside him. No Ellie. The door creaked. There she was…the woman who'd made him feel whole again. No wonder none of his other relationships had worked out. She toed the door open. 'Ah! You made coffee! You're an angel.'

'A crazy-haired angel.' Ellie grinned, handing him a steaming mug, adding, 'White and two.'

He pushed himself up to sitting, loving the way her light cotton dressing gown fluttered across her curves as she crossed the room to toe open the French doors. 'I just want to keep an eye out for Mav,' she explained.

'Will he be back before he heads off to surf school?'

'Not always. Mum usually sends a text if she's bringing him round, but there's been nothing so far today.'

He took a draught of the coffee. 'Delicious.' He caught her hand in his as she settled in the space next to him on the bed then gave the back of it a kiss. 'Just like you.'

When he looked up at her, he saw she was frowning.

'What's wrong? Don't like being called delicious?'

'No, it's not that.' She gave his arm a rub, her frown softening into something a bit less worried looking. 'I just… Do you think Mav should know about…you know…' she pointed at the two of them '…us?'

'I suppose that depends on where you see this going.' He was going to give her the lead on this. He had to.

'Step by step. Super slowly,' she said with a decisive nod.

'Sounds good.' It did. As he'd learnt, the very best of things were worth waiting for. He scooched over beneath the duvet so they were side by side. 'Does that include more Mummy and Daddy time?'

She giggled and swotted at the air. 'It's so weird to hear you say that.'

'What? Mummy and Daddy?'

'Yeah.' Her nose crinkled up, but she was still smiling.

'It's what we are.'

'It's what we are *now*,' she reminded him as she put her coffee down on the bedside table. 'Ish.'

He put his mug down on the other side

table and climbed out from under the light down covers so that he was sitting astride her legs. He took both of her hands and placed them on his chest. 'Feel that?'

She waited a moment, then nodded after the thump-thump of his heartbeat registered. 'Yup.'

'That's all yours. Yours and Mav's.' He leant in and gave her a deep, hungry kiss, her hands still pressed to his heart. 'Feel that?'

Her grin widened. 'I hope that's not for Mav.'

'Nope! That's just for you.' He sat back on his heels. 'It's always been there, Ells. That heartbeat. And I think you feel the same way.'

'What? All tachycardic?' She grinned. 'I'm far too cool for that nonsense.'

'Oh, yeah?' He began to tickle her. Tickle and kiss and nuzzle and play until before he knew it, the two of them were naked again— laughing, touching, kissing, caressing—until once again their lovemaking culminated in a climax that shot the pair of them into the stratosphere.

Lucas fell back on to the bed after their breathing had steadied. 'Well, that was fun.'

'You make it fun.' She poked him with a toe, then picked up her coffee mug.

'Fun like last night fun or fun like carnival fun?'

She pushed her lips out and gave him a studied look over the rim of her lukewarm coffee. 'Mmm…last night wasn't really fun, it was more…' she lowered her voice to a sexy growl '…luxurious. Slow and yummy. Like the way you'd want to enjoy a very, very special box of Christmas truffles.'

He could get on board with this line of thinking. 'Could you get used to having something that decadent on a more regular basis?'

She hesitated before answering. 'Was this what you imagined happening when you came down here? Slipping into my bed after a long day of saving pets' lives?'

It was a fair question. One that deserved an honest answer. But just then the door was bashed open and standing in the bedroom doorway, looking completely bewildered, was Maverick.

Ellie yelped and pulled the duvet up more snugly around her. 'Mav! Hey, there, love.'

'Morning, Mummy.' He looked at Lucas next. 'Hello, Lucas.'

Hmm… Sometimes he was Daddy. Sometimes he was Lucas. Lucas mostly when he wasn't sure about something.

'Morning, Mav. Your mum and I were just—'

'Talking about the day's surgical rota,' Ellie cut in with a cheery grin.

'In bed?' Maverick clearly thought that was a ridiculous place to talk about work.

Ellie threw Lucas a *fix this now* look.

'Absolutely. Did you know that the brain is most creative in the morning?'

'Is that why you always get up before me, Mummy?'

Lucas seemed to be buying the explanation.

'It's one of the reasons, love. Um… Do you mind throwing me that T-shirt over there? And the skirt?'

Lucas bit back a laugh as Maverick handed her the items with a bemused expression.

She wriggled into them with rather amusing efficiency, flipped back the covers then threw Lucas the fresh pair of scrubs they'd brought up from the surgery unit last night that had never quite made it onto his body.

'Pancakes?' she asked.

'Love 'em.' He grinned his thanks.

This, he thought with a smile, could well be the perfect start to a proper family life.

A few stacks of pancakes, lashings of maple syrup and several glasses of orange juice later, Ellie breathed a sigh of relief. Lucas had stayed for breakfast but excused himself to make some phone calls for the clinic whilst Ellie and Mav sorted out the day pack he took to camp. Throughout it all? No one mentioned anything about Mummy and Daddy under the covers.

After clearing the table, Ellie ran a comb through her son's unruly mop and then gave him a kiss on the forehead.

He looked up at her, his eyes wide and hopeful. 'Is Lucas going to stay here now?'

Lucas, not Daddy.

Ellie's face froze in a cheery Mummy face as she tried to figure out the best way to answer that.

Maybe?

Probably not?

Not until they had a proper talk about things anyway. And ensured she'd got over the fact he'd proposed, taken it back then at least seemed to have swanned off to live a highly glamorous life without her. He'd explained that part pretty well, but…it didn't mean what had happened still didn't sting. And there was also her guilt about not telling Lucas about Maverick and the fact she'd have to explain that to her son one day.

Not really the simplest of answers for a five-year-old.

'Come here, bub.' She pulled her son into a little half-hug and touched her finger to the tip of his nose. 'Mummy and Daddy are figuring out how things are going to work around here. It's been a while since they've seen each other and I'm pretty used to how things worked with Uncle Drew.'

'Uncle Drew never spends the night with you.'

'Very true.' She gave a serious nod instead of giggling. As if! She'd made sandcastles with Uncle Drew. And mud pies. He was like a brother to her. And an awesome business partner. Not to mention a pretty great vet. But kissing him? Bleurgh. 'But Uncle Drew and I never dated.'

'You and Daddy did?'

'We did. During vet school. And then he had to go and be the Uber-Vet for a few years.'

It was sort of a white lie. More a lie of omission than an actual lie, so...

'Like superheroes have to go and save the world?'

She smiled, wishing Lucas was here to hear this. 'Yeah. A bit like that. So...now that he's not fixing all the animals on telly, he's thinking about what he'd like to do next.'

'Why doesn't he work here?'

'Well…'

'There are all sorts of animals he could fix here,' Maverick said, the idea clearly growing on him. 'All the puppies and Mrs Cartwright's cat and the animals in the petting zoo and…um… Moose! He could fix Moose.'

'Moose could definitely do with some Uber-Vet magic.' Moose was also one of the reasons Ellie hadn't sent Lucas packing. The Bernese mountain dog had suffered some fairly awful injuries in a car accident and Ellie had been hoping Henry might be able to work his magic. Since he'd left, Lucas had had a couple of appointments with him, certain he could help. He'd said prosthetics were possible for the large canine, but that he had something even more ground-breaking in mind.

'If he wants to fix the animals in Dolphin Cove,' Maverick began slowly, avoiding eye contact, 'would he live here like other daddies?'

'Well…' It was a valid question. Particularly from a five-year-old who had been pretty awesome about accepting a previously entirely absent father into his life.

'Not all mummies and daddies sleep in the same bed every night.'

'You mean like I change my cuddly toys around sometimes?'

'Sort of.' Ellie crossed to the sink and pretended to be really busy washing dishes for a minute.

She was on the brink of asking Mav how he would feel if Lucas were to stay around longer term when her son pulled on his snorkel and mask then patted his round tummy. 'I'm ready to hit the waves.'

Ah! The magical mindset of a five-year-old.

'I hope they're good ones today.'

Maverick made a sad face. 'Only one more week before school starts.'

'I know, bub.' She gave his curly head another scrub. 'But you love it there. Learning all sorts of cool things is one of the perks of growing up.' Ellie knelt in front of him and gave each of his pudgy cheeks a kiss then waved him off as he ran down the steps just as Lucas reappeared from the clinic.

Maverick launched himself off the stairs towards Lucas before he'd reached the bottom of the steps. Ellie was about to scream when, as if he'd been doing it all his life, Lucas swept his son up in his arms and whirled him round and round to Maverick's complete and utter delight.

The pair of them looked up at her and grinned. In that moment Ellie knew she wanted Lucas to stay. She was ready to love him again. Really love him the way she once had. Maverick deserved it. She deserved it. And, from the sound of what Lucas had gone through with his family, he deserved some happiness, too.

An hour later the pair of them had barely laid eyes on one another the clinic was so busy. When she ran into him in the surgical unit her heart softened rather than raced. A sign, she realised, that her fear about him leaving was dissipating.

'Ooh.' She gave the supine feline in his arms a stroke. 'This isn't Mrs Cartwright's, is it?'

'No.' Lucas held up the chart. 'This is Shadow.'

'Oh, right.' She scanned the chart. 'The Thomases' cat. Everything okay?'

'She'll be fine. A bit of periodontal disease. I'm thinking too much tinned tuna might be the culprit.'

'SCC?'

He tapped the side of his nose.

'Ouch. How many teeth did you have to extract?'

'Just one. The family noticed her eating habits had changed and of course...'

'Halitosis,' they said together.

'Luckily, they caught it before things got too bad. And they've promised to change her feeding so, fingers crossed, all will be well.'

'Speaking of too much seafood.' Ellie pointed at Lord Fluffingstein, who was giving the pair of them lots of doleful brown-eyed looks. 'Any chance you could help me escort the crab-lover here into the waiting room?'

'Ah! Are his family here?'

'Yup. From the second the clinic opened, bless 'em.'

'Excellent.' He rubbed his hands together. 'I love a good reunion, me.'

Ellie smiled. 'Course you do, you big ol' soppy thing.'

'Who're you calling soppy?' Lucas play-protested, already clearing his throat at the thought of the family being reunited with their cherished dog. It was one of the reasons she'd fallen for him so fast. His genuine affection for the animals they treated was infectious.

After ensuring his post-surgical shirt was snapped into place, Lucas and Ellie slowly escorted Lord Fluffingstein down the corridor for the inevitable tearful reunion. Ellie gave instructions to the family for the dog's post-operative care. 'He'll be a little dopey for the next day or two as the anaesthetic wears off.' She handed over a small bag. 'These are his medicines. Some for pain and some to ensure any infection is kept at bay. Keeping the wound area clean is critical for the next few days so no beach time, I'm afraid.'

They all shook their heads soberly. 'We've got a garden in our holiday let so we'll just use that.'

'Excellent. In a few days he should be all right to travel home, and we will make sure to send along all the information to your local vets.'

The mum threw herself at Ellie and pulled her into a huge hug. 'Thank you so much for saving our boy. He's like another son to me and if we'd lost him...' A sob escaped her lips.

'It's all right,' Ellie soothed, returning the hug. 'He's alive and well and will continue to have a happy healthy life as long as he avoids lead weights and the wound stays clean.'

'It'll be the cleanest wound in Britain,' the family's little girl solemnly vowed, holding up her fingers in a Girl Guide salute.

'Well, then,' Lucas said, kneeling down so that he was at eye level with her. 'I shall look forward to receiving pictures of his stitches when they're all healed up. Here…' He pulled out his phone. 'Who wants my email address so they can send me updates?'

The entire family raised their hands and Lord Fluffingstein gave a soft woof.

Ellie laughed, happy and relieved to finally be able to enjoy her time with Lucas. Being on her guard for the past few weeks had been exhausting. It had added a level of fatigue she hadn't needed on top of all the extra work she'd been juggling at the clinic. Despite her best efforts, she yawned.

'Long night?' asked the father.

Lucas smiled. 'I kept her up late.'

Ellie raised her eyebrows until Lucas smoothly finished, 'We were doing some in-depth debriefing after the surgery, you see. We're all about a hands-on approach here. Seeing things through to a happy ending.'

He slipped his arm around her shoulder in what, to the Lab's family, would have looked like an ordinary gesture of happy colleagues, but to Ellie? The gesture and his words meant the world. Maybe Mummy and Daddy could sleep in the same bed on a more regular basis. And not at all like Maverick's cuddly toys.

CHAPTER EIGHT

'FANCY A REAL PINT?' Lucas picked up his empty glass and reached across for Drew's drained soft-drink glass.

'No, mate. Thanks. Painkillers,' he explained.

As if he had to. The poor guy had clearly been through the wringer. Drew lived in a cottage a short walk from the Hungry Pelican, but it had taken him a painstaking twenty minutes to hobble his way down. A walk he'd insisted on when Lucas had shown up in his big old four-by-four that wouldn't even begin to fit in the narrow lanes of the medieval village.

Pins and braces and goodness knew what else were holding Drew together. Grit and determination, most likely.

'Another plate of chips wouldn't go amiss, though!'

'They know how to do them right here at

the Pelican, don't they?' Lucas said, swinging his legs out of the booth and heading towards the bar.

After a quick exchange with Ellie's father, whose protective demeanour had become less frosty as the summer wore on, Lucas was back in the booth, enjoying his long-awaited catch-up with Drew.

'And things with Ellie are cool?' Drew asked.

Lucas gave a definitive nod. 'Far better than I could've dreamt. Maverick's…' His voice grew rough and he gave the table a thump. 'He's one helluva kid.'

'Damn straight he is. He has the best uncle in the whole of England for starters.' Drew said proudly. His mood turned serious as he retained solid eye contact. 'I'm glad things are cool with you and Ellie. I have to admit I was worried when she rang to say you'd offered Henry your job and were coming down to replace him. It felt like—' He stopped himself.

'What?' Lucas had a feeling Drew had just stopped himself from delivering a home truth. Something along the lines of 'It felt like you were taking matters into your own hands again'. He'd never looked at it that way. He'd decided on Ellie's behalf what she would do.

The grain of truth was a reminder that just because things were okay now, they might not always be. Life threw spanners into the works. It didn't mean you had to deal with them alone. Ellie hadn't. She had an amazing support system here. She'd been strong enough to admit she'd needed help.

Drew squinted at him then said, 'I don't want to see Ellie hurt again. Or Mav.'

'They won't be,' Lucas said, the words weighted with intent.

Drew gave him a nod. 'You made it extra-tough, staging your comeback when I was in traction.'

'Tough how?'

'It's hard to give someone a black eye from a hospital bed.' The familiar glimmer of fun flared in Drew's eyes as he gave Lucas a shake of his fist.

Lucas snorted. 'I'm on good behaviour alert.'

'But it's water under the bridge now?' Drew couldn't keep the protective note out of his voice. 'If it isn't, or if you hurt her again, you know I'm going to have to run you out of town. Slowly. But I'll do it.'

'I believe you,' Lucas assured him. And he did. Half the village would most likely join him, pitchforks and all. Ellie was one of their own and, famous or not, Lucas was an outsider. An outsider who'd broken the heart of one of the village's favourite daughters. 'I swear to you, mate, my intentions are entirely honourable. And I know I messed up. Things with my family were... They were pretty rough there for a bit.'

'I would ask you if you wanted to talk about it, but...' Drew held his hands out. 'I'm a bloke.'

Lucas laughed. 'Yeah, right. You're probably cuddling up to your cat every night, yapping on about feelings all night with a weepy film on in the background.'

'Sorry, pal.' Drew tugged a hand through his dark hair. 'Books over telly and I don't have any pets.'

'What?' Lucas was genuinely shocked. 'A vet without a pet. That's weird.'

Drew fixed Lucas with a *Shall we look in the mirror?* stare. 'Do you have any?'

Lucas shifted uncomfortably in his seat. Esmerelda was meant to have been his and Ellie's dog. The idea of getting another one... especially with his insane work schedule... even a goldfish would've been neglected. 'Maybe I was choosing the wrong barometer to judge you by.'

Drew waved away the comment. 'I couldn't have a dog now. Not with the way I'm walking.' He feigned some creaky walking frame noises.

'You'll get there. Like everything, it takes time.'

Drew looked away but not before Lucas saw a lance of pain cross his features. Emotional pain this time. Whether it was the car crash or losing his fiancée a couple of years back, Lucas didn't know, neither did he press. He was going to be around for the foreseeable future, and he knew Drew would talk when he was good and ready. Which reminded him. 'You really think you're going to be ready to come back to work?'

A look of determination pushed Drew to an upright position. 'I've let Ellie down enough these past few weeks. I'll be coming back at the end of September, as promised.'

'You've not let her down in the slightest. She knows you didn't ask your brakes to fail.'

That same shadowed look darkened Drew's blue eyes a second time. 'Yeah, well. It's not fair on her. All the extra work she's taken on.'

'About that…' Lucas began.

'What?' Drew laughed. 'Are you volunteering to stay on?'

Lucas would've preferred to talk to Ellie about it first, but...maybe it was wise to test the waters. 'Yes. If it would help.'

'Always the hero, aren't you?'

The comment slashed through any chumminess they might've had. Drew didn't trust him to stay.

Lucas's gaze sharpened. 'What makes you say that?'

'Sorry, mate. These meds I'm on don't give me much room for charm. I— Oh, hell.' He dropped his head into his hands, gave his skull a brisk rub and then looked Drew straight in the eye. 'Mate, it didn't seem very *you* to dump me and Ellie—mostly Ellie. We'd planned to set the clinic up together. When we saw you swanning around on those red carpets with that woman on your arm—'

'She was my producer!' Lucas said forcefully, too late to dial his tone back to contrition. 'There was never anything between us. Not on my part anyway. And after that, well...anyone else you saw would've been me trying to convince myself I'd moved on.'

'So, you still love her, then? Ellie?' he added, as if there was anyone else in the world they could be talking about.

Lucas nodded. Of course he did. Always

had somewhere beneath that weighted cloak of family responsibility he'd put on six years back.

'Any plans to…you know?' Drew wiggled his ring finger in the air.

Lucas gave his jaw a scrub. 'I don't think we're quite there yet, mate.' Winning Ellie's full trust was of paramount importance and until he had it he was going to play his cards close to his chest. Well…pretty close.

'Fair enough.' Drew gave his hands a decisive clap as if the matter had been discussed, settled and need never more be revisited. He put out his hand for a shake, any friction between them now laid to rest. Lucas took it with gratitude.

Drew and Ellie had been his best friends back in the day. They'd known his father had been unwell. That his brother liked one drink too many. Why hadn't he reached out to them?

Pride.

Fear.

Powerful enemies at a time of crisis.

Drew took a studied sip of his soft drink then said, 'About the clinic. I'm going mad over there in the cottage doing nothing so… talk me through what a man who's hobbling about can do to ease the load.'

'Get better,' Lucas said solidly. And then, 'Actually, do you remember Ellie telling you about a Bernese mountain dog Henry had scheduled for a prosthetics op? Moose?'

'Moose!' Drew's expression visibly lightened. 'I love that big old bear of a dog.' His brow furrowed. 'Has he not done well? Ellie hasn't told me much about any of the cases.'

Lucas could see why when it came to Moose. The poor dog had been hit by a car careening out of control and had nearly died. She'd done her best with his internal injuries, but his 'rear legs cart' wasn't really up to the job of helping him lead a normal healthy life.

'Henry had planned to give him two prosthetic legs, but I have another idea.'

Drew's face lit up. 'Tell me everything.'

The two friends spent the next hour talking over the case, possible options and then moved on to the actual business of how the clinic was running.

'I think you could do with another full-time vet. One who could come with a cash injection.'

Drew raised his eyebrows. 'Only partners give cash injections.'

'Yup. I know. I've been thinking about ways to show Ellie I'm here for the long run and I thought it might be a good show of faith.

Would you be happy if I were to propose—'
He stopped himself and changed his choice
of words. 'Would you be happy if I were to
ask to become a partner?'

'I'm happy if Ellie's happy.'

'Excellent.' He lifted his pint glass and
Drew raised his soft drink. 'Cheers to that,
mate. To new beginnings.'

Drew pulled his glass back an inch. 'Aren't
you getting a bit ahead of yourself?'

'Maybe,' Lucas agreed. 'But you can't
blame a man for wanting to be part of one of
the best clinics in the land, can you?'

'Not for a second, mate,' Drew said, letting his glass clink against Lucas's. 'Not for
a second.'

'One…two…three…*go!*'

Ellie, Lucas and Maverick started cheering
and calling their puppies.

'C'mon, little one! You can do it!'

'Here, Mr Purple! Come to me. No! Not
Mummy, me! Mav!'

'Come to Papa, Miss Green!'

Ellie shot Lucas a glance. *Come to Papa?*
She snorted as the little golden Lab pranced
towards him then veered off to climb up the
slide.

When the little chocolate Lab she'd chosen

for the race, landed on Ellie's lap first, Lucas pronounced them the winners. She was a gorgeous little thing. Getting big. She was also astonishingly obedient for a young pup. She gave her head a little stroke. Perhaps Drew might like—

'Mum!'

She looked up and realised Lucas and Maverick were both staring at her. 'Sorry. Yes?'

'Can I take Lucas to the petting zoo? I want to introduce him to Barnacle. Maybe we could take him for a swim?'

Lucas raised his eyebrows and gave her an inquisitive look. 'Barnacle?'

'He's our resident buck goat. He should also be a contender for the Olympic swimming team. He loves it.' She nodded at his untucked shirt. 'You'll want to watch that. He eats anything. And by anything I mean anything.'

Maverick nodded intensely. 'She's not lying. The reason we have him is because where he used to live he ate all of their laundry.'

Ellie smiled and ruffled her son's hair. 'Maybe not all of the laundry, but let's say Barnacle's former owners would've been wise not to keep him in the back garden.'

Maverick put his hand in hers. 'Will Lucas be coming to school with us next week?'

'Oh!' She glanced across at Lucas, who suddenly busied himself with getting the puppies back into their pen. 'Well...' Most of the villagers had figured out Lucas and Maverick's relationship as the pair of them looked so similar and her mother refusing to confirm or deny whenever people nipped into the pub to 'casually enquire'.

'Would you like him to come?'

'Yes,' Maverick said. 'And you, too,' he added, his little forehead crinkling as he waited for her answer.

Lucas cleared his throat then turned to them. 'I'd be honoured. As long as you're happy.' The last part was obviously for Ellie.

'Sure,' she said, in a much higher voice than her normal one. 'That'd be great!'

'And can he come to the Christmas play, too? Last year I was a star and this year I want to be a sheep. Or a donkey!'

Lucas laughed, but Ellie could see the questions in his eyes. The same ones she was asking herself. Would he be here in December? Would she want him here?

'C'mon! Let's go get Barnacle,' Maverick tugged on Lucas's hand, the topic clearly not important enough to decide upon now. Thank goodness.

She waved the pair of them off after Lucas

promised he'd be back after dropping Mav off with her parents for the afternoon so he could get to the surgery.

As she watched them head off to the small petting zoo, two blond heads, one big hand holding one little hand, Mav skip-running to keep up with his father's long strides, her heart near enough burst. As much as she was loth to admit it, she loved having Lucas here, watching him with Mav. He was brilliant with him—surprise, surprise.

A soft smile hit her lips as she remembered the way he'd run into the ocean with all of his clothes on the other day when Maverick had come off his boogie board and given himself a proper friction burn. Never mind the fact she'd been a nanosecond ahead of him. Knowing Lucas's instincts when it came to Mav were the same as hers made her feel complete in a way she'd never felt before. As if having both parents there to look after her boy had filled an emptiness she hadn't realised needed filling.

But would this be enough for him? It was summer in Cornwall. What wasn't to love? Sun, sand, surf...the odd foray between the sheets with an ex-lover... But what about when the rains came? Lambing season. A cranky little boy refusing to get up on dark mornings for an early start at school. Summertime in Dolphin Cove was 'bed of roses' territory. Not reality. Even the sleeping-together part. That was the pair of them caught up in some absurd lust bubble that would no doubt pop when the clocks went back and Lucas headed off to whatever it was he was going to do next.

And that was the crux of it. Instead of believing he'd be around for ever as Mav was, there was a part of her still wondering when he would pack his bags and go.

She gave the pup a final cuddle then made a solemn vow.

Until Lucas told her what he was going to do after his stint here, she needed to keep her heart firmly under control.

'So this is your big plan?' Ellie looked across at Lucas, who had just finished drawing on the Bernese mountain dog's X-rays. When she saw his big ear-to-ear smile, she couldn't help but grin, too.

'Yup!' Lucas was excited. Kid in a sweet shop excited. 'Drew likes it, too.'

Ellie swotted at his arm. 'You told Drew before you told me?'

'Well…' He slipped an arm along her waist and lowered his voice and his lips until they were brushing against her ear. 'I would've told you last night after I got back from seeing him, but someone was feeling a little bit naughty.'

'It takes two to tango, *mate*,' she said primly, then, unable to resist, gave his bum a quick squeeze as she glanced over her shoulder at the door.

You never knew when one of the surgical nurses would pop in to check up on things. Ever since Lucas had arrived there had been quite a lot of spontaneous 'popping in to check on things'. Something they'd learnt to be hyper-vigilant about once sneaking the odd kiss had appeared on the agenda. She knew it wasn't really the best way to steel her heart against him but…once he left who knew how long it would be until she had sex again?

Because of that, each morning after they untangled themselves from one another she would remind herself. *This doesn't mean anything…nothing definite anyway.*

Either way, for the time being, she felt happy. Warily happy but… Work. Play. They were all melding into one and it felt lovely after so much stress with getting the business up and running and then poor Drew's accident. When she was being really, properly honest with herself, she knew that the past couple of weeks had been just like…her breath caught in her throat…falling in love.

'Ells…' Lucas's tone had changed. 'I want to talk about something.'

'What? Is everything all right at home?'

'Yes, fine.'

Adrenaline charged through her. 'Has Mav's surf school rung?'

'No, no. Don't worry, he's fine. It's Drew.'

'Drew?' Her hands flew to her heart. 'Has something happened?'

'He's worried about you.'

'What? Why? I'm the one who should be worried about him.' She started hammering Lucas with questions about Drew, his emotional state, his eating habits, his leg. Lucas answered them the best he could, but Ellie persisted. She should've seen him more. Made more of an effort to pull him out of this funk. 'Did you get the impression he was walking as much as he should? Whenever Mav and I have gone over, he's never mentioned it.' An idea struck. 'I was thinking of giving him one of Esmerelda's puppies. The chocolate one.'

'What? Are you sure he could handle a puppy? He's going to be on crutches for weeks yet.'

Ellie waved his concerns away. 'The pups

are almost ready to leave their mother now. In fact…' She did a quick tot up on her fingers. 'This is perfect. It gives Drew time to develop a bond with his puppy and will mean he has a chance to get out and about with her before he's threatening to come back at the end of September.' And you're due to leave.

'Desk duty?' Lucas checked.

'Desk duty,' Ellie confirmed, then dared to voice a deepening concern. 'He shouldn't even be coming back then, but I thought I'd better have a plan in place if he showed up. No way am I letting him anywhere near the surgical unit.' They spoke for a while longer about ensuring they visited him more, sending Mav over with a basket of some of his favourite things from the bakery and the pub—he'd always been a sucker for Wyn's fishfinger sandwiches—and, of course, to play board games. Cool Uncle Drew was the only human on earth who had enough patience to play games with Maverick for hours on end.

'Sounds like a plan,' Ellie said, pleased someone else was helping her lure Drew out of his man cave. She glanced over at the wall clock. 'I'd better get back to the main building. There's a list of patients as long as my arm coming in for afternoon clinic.' She stifled a yawn. She'd never admit it, but she couldn't wait for Drew to come back. And maybe a locum. If they could afford it.

'Ellie.' Lucas stopped her. 'Drew and I also talked about the fact that I think you—and by "you" I mean the clinic—need more help. There's too much work for the two of you and definitely too much for one.'

She rolled her eyes. 'More help' had been a recurring theme in her life for the last six years. 'And where exactly are we going to get the money to pay for this much-needed help?'

He gave her one of his cheesy Uber-Vet grins. 'You're looking at it, baby.'

What? Was he offering to stay?

'Oh, Lucas…it's a big commitment.'

'Yes, I know. And along the same lines we need to discuss Maverick.'

She stiffened. 'What about him?'

'I know we haven't discussed visits or anything, but…'

Here it was. The request for joint custody.

'I'd like to move here. Permanently.'

Her hearing began to feel fuzzy. 'Where, here?' Like…into her flat here?

'Dolphin Cove. I'd like to buy into the partnership.'

Her heart didn't know what to do with itself. Squeeze tight. Sink. Pound with joy?

It wasn't a marriage proposal. It was a business proposal. It was Lucas playing it safe.

Just like she'd asked him to.

So why did she feel sad?

Because maybe a little bit she did want him to ask her to marry him?

Would that be enough? Working together? Sharing Mav's care? Raising him together, but...no relationship? Not a romantic one anyway.

She instantly regretted the regular habit of lovemaking they'd fallen into far too easily. If he lived here permanently, she didn't want him as a friend with benefits. It was too intimate if something went wrong. So what did she want him to be? Her husband? Really? After all they'd been through?

She stared at him. Hard.

And then it hit her.

When it came to Lucas Williams she wanted the whole package or nothing at all. But now that he knew about Maverick, Lucas would have to be in her life. One way or another. And it looked as though he wanted it to be on the business end of things. She swore under her breath. Guess that lust bubble had well and truly popped.

'Ells?'

'I don't know, Lucas.' She looked anywhere but at him.

'Don't give me an answer yet.' He ducked down to try and catch her eye. Intimate contact she really wanted to avoid right now. 'It's a lot to think about. Why don't you take the next couple of weeks and if you need more time, I'll hang on as long as you need?'

She didn't need two weeks. Having him here on a daily basis, believing they'd grown closer than ever, it had all been a lie she'd told herself. A stupid dream she'd clung to all these years.

'We don't have the funding for that, Lucas. Once Drew comes back, the insurance—'

'I'll work free. And Caro will as well. For the project on Moose anyway.'

She finally met his gaze, utterly confused. 'Who?'

'Caro Barnes. The inventor who drew up these plans.' He pointed at the roll of sheets they'd just been poring over. 'Remember? My contact from the Uber-Vet days.'

Ellie glanced at them, the complications doubling as she did so.

Of course she wanted him to do the surgery. Moose deserved nothing less than the very best. She also wanted Lucas to stay on at the clinic. Her brain did anyway. It more than made sense, but her gut? It wanted to send Lucas packing right now so she could go back to life the way it had been before Drew's horrid accident.

'I don't know...'

'Oh, c'mon, Ells,' Lucas persisted, clearly oblivious to her emotional turmoil. 'How is this any different from the students you've had down from uni or having Henry here? The Dolphin Cove Veterinary Clinic already has a great reputation for pushing the envelope. You should be pulling in the big guns and, let me tell you, Caro is one of them.'

It's not about her, you idiot. It's about you.

'How do you know her again?'

'She used to work for a really innovative robotics company out in California. They helped us with a couple of tricky cases on the show.'

She tuned in a bit more. Relationship problems aside, Lucas did have some amazing contacts. If he could persuade more of them to come down for special cases like Moose's, the clinic's reputation would grow.

'Did the robotics work?'

'Absolutely. There was some trial and error, but if you want someone who thrives on burning the midnight oil to see an idea through,

Caro's your girl. And, double bonus, she's right down the road.'

'In Cornwall? Why's she here?'

Lucas shook his head. 'Not sure. Something about breaking free to work on her own ideas outside the corporate machine, I think. She's not exactly super-chatty. Neither is she asking for a pay cheque.'

Weird. 'Doesn't she need money?'

'Eventually. But for now Caro wants to see if this will work. She's an inventor. Trialling something experimental is a key step in making those giant leaps.'

Ellie nodded. Bringing Caro on board for trial treatments would be a real boon for them. More to the point, having Lucas Williams—aka the Uber-Vet—at the surgery would be about a hundred times more amazing. Famous or not, he was a brilliant vet. Always had been. He'd always been able to put two things together other veterinarians didn't have the guts for. He was a thinker, whereas she was a reactor, which was why emergencies were her forte. So…if she was coming at this whole 'I want to be a partner' thing from Drew's perspective? It'd be stupid to send him packing. At this point anyway. Especially if Moose had a chance at a normal life. Drew would go mad for that type of surgery.

'Okay. I'm happy to give the go-ahead for Caro. Start small, aim high, right?'

Lucas grinned. 'It's how the best dreams come true.' He pulled a few sheaves out of the drawings tube and handed them to her. 'Let's take another look at these, shall we?'

Ah. The clinic.

Despite her muddied emotions, she was drawn into the fascinating proposal.

'They look like architectural drawings.'

'They are in a way.' Lucas helped her spread the large papers out on the surgical table.

'It's all very modern.'

'Robotic legs usually are.'

Ellie shot him a goofy smile. 'I don't mean that, it's just…there aren't that many dogs wandering round the planet with robotic legs.'

'Good point. Although there is a Rottweiler over in the States who's got four.'

'He had four leg amputations?' Caro was shocked. 'What happened to him?'

'Frostbite. His owner kept him outside in sub-zero temperatures and—'

Ellie stopped him. 'Don't. I can't even imagine a dog being treated that way.'

They spent a few minutes poring over the details and when she finally felt she had her head wrapped around the concept she stretched and grinned. 'I think it'll be brilliant. Do you want to call Moose's owners or shall I?'

'Your clinic…'

'Your patient,' she countered, knowing she would have to make a decision soon as to whether or not she'd like it to be his clinic, too.

Maybe she did need those couple of weeks to think about it after all.

A couple of days later Lucas found himself being dragged to the whelping pen for some puppy time with Maverick. Willingly escorted was a better description, Lucas thought as Maverick pushed through the swinging doors into the puppy unit. He had a million things to do to prep for the robotic leg surgery the following week, but if he'd learnt anything over the past few weeks, it was that time was precious and if his son wanted him to spend ten minutes playing with puppies he'd find that ten minutes come hell or high water.

As for the surgical prep, that's what coffee was for.

'Which one's your favourite?' Maverick asked.

Lucas, who was sitting in the middle of the

pen and being used as a climbing frame by the rambunctious pups, gave the puppies a considered scan. 'Depends on what you want the puppy for, I guess. Most of these are going to be trained to be therapy dogs, right?'

Maverick nodded, his face very earnest, as if he took responsibility for the dogs and their futures himself. 'Hearing dogs. Therapy dogs. They do all sorts.'

'Esmerelda's an amazing mummy to have all these lovely puppies, isn't she?'

Maverick nodded happily. 'Esmerelda's the best. She's going to come and live up in the flat again soon.'

'Once the puppies are weaned?'

Maverick gave a solid little-boy nod. 'Mummy is going to get all of the puppy carers to come over then. Then they'll all be gone.' He stroked a little black Lab who jumped up and licked him on the nose. Mav's expression turned gloomy. 'I know they're going to lovely places and that they will be helping people, but…'

'But what?'

Mav choked back a small sob. 'I'd like it better if they could stay.' He looked up at Lucas, threads of anxiety woven across his cute little-boy face. Lucas couldn't bear it.

He knew what Maverick was really asking. Would Lucas be leaving, too?

Lucas pulled his son onto his lap along with Mav's favourite puppy, Mr Purple, a golden Lab with a black button nose and a little purple collar to differentiate him from the others. Lucas knew he could spot his boy in a crowd of thousands of blonds. He held him close, so grateful to Ellie for having raised a son who was kind, smart, inquisitive, funny and just about everything a man could ever dream of. He owed her a debt of gratitude he would spend his life repaying.

'I know the puppies have to leave. It's part of growing up, but…' Oh, this was tricky territory. Territory he really should cover with Ellie first. 'How would you feel if I were to stay longer?'

Maverick whirled round in Lucas's lap, the puppy tumbling back into the jumble of happy furballs. 'Are you going to stay?'

'I'd like to. I'd like it very much.'

Maverick whooped with joy and threw his arms round Lucas's neck. Lucas wasn't a crier, but it was hard to focus with tears swimming in his eyes. This was a moment he would cherish for ever.

A movement caught his eye.

Ellie.

She was standing in the doorway and from the look on her face had been listening to their conversation. Her eyes glistened with tears. Was this it? The sign he'd been waiting for that Ellie had forgiven him?

Maverick scooped up Mr Purple. 'What about Marvin?'

Ellie began to giggle, crossing to join them. 'Marvin? I thought we were going to wait for the puppy carers to give them names.'

Mav looked at her like she was missing half her brain. 'This one's definitely Marvin.' He shot his mother an impish look. 'He's an Uber puppy! And he told me he'd like to stay with us. In the flat. Not next door.' His eyes darted to Lucas then to his mother, his eyes in full *Please, please, Mummy, can we?* mode.

Bash.

Lucas's heart was going to be bruised to a pulp if things continued in this vein. Bruising he could totally get used to.

To her credit, and obvious skill as a mum used to receiving her son's wide-eyed appeals, she laughed and gave Marvin a little scrub on the head. 'All in good time.' She popped her mouth into an O as if an idea had struck. 'Why don't you, me and Lucas all head down to the beach tonight? Have a barbecue before the sunny days start drawing in?'

Mav clapped his hands, a life with Marvin temporarily forgotten. 'Can we have marshmallows?'

Ellie nodded. 'Absolutely. And sausages. And...' Her sparkling green eyes shifted to Lucas. 'What do you like?'

'You,' he said.

Her cheeks flamed hot and bright. 'Well, of course you do. I'm fabulous.' Then she turned on her heel, muttering something about needing to see to a pregnant hamster.

Lucas grinned. She would come round. In time. And time was something he had oodles of.

CHAPTER NINE

THE CLINIC WAS absolutely buzzing with excitement. Today was the day Moose would finally receive his prosthesis. News Ellie was quite certain her mother had spread rather liberally round the village.

Once he had healed and was trialling his robotic legs along the beach and in the countryside, who knew what sort of crowd they'd draw?

To steady her nerves, Ellie took extra care in the scrub room, watching through the glass window as the operating theatre filled with staff, all equally charged up to change the Bernese mountain dog's life.

She and Lucas had had several meetings with Caro over the past week, but she'd opted not to come down to the clinic for the actual surgery, even though Ellie had assured her she was welcome.

She was a quirky one, Caro Barnes. Model-gorgeous, she was all flowing blonde hair and lean athletic body—a proper California girl—but she liked her own space and, from the sound of her working schedule, her own style of timekeeping. She'd mentioned looking out at the shooting stars late at night more than once when asked to explain how she'd come up with this or that idea.

Ellie gave her arms a final scrub then wove her way through the surgical nurses so that she and Lucas were on opposite sides of the operating table where Moose was still awake, happily receiving the adoration of the chief surgical nurse.

'You ready?' she asked Lucas.

The crinkles by his eyes fanned out above his surgical mask. 'As I'll ever be.'

Ellie grinned. She was absolutely fizzing with excitement. More than ever, the past few days had felt exactly as they had back in the day when they'd poured big mugs of coffee or hot chocolate and hit the books and their laptops, researching everything they could to make sure the complex surgery they were about to do went well.

They'd agreed to put the question of whether or not Lucas should become a partner on hold because what they were about to do warranted their full attention.

'Have you told the *Dolphin Cove Gazette*?' Lucas teased. 'I've never seen the reception area so full.'

'In Dolphin Cove, there's no need. Especially if Mum knows what we're up to.' Ellie laughed. 'You should see the beach!' A warm fuzzy feeling filled her heart. 'It's happened a few times when one of the village's favourite pets was about to have their life changed. The family needs support, and we all just pull together when the going gets tough.'

A few weeks back Lucas would've winced at something like that. This time? Ellie was relieved to see him smile and nod and say, 'As it should be.'

'Right, everyone.' He got the busy surgical room's attention. 'Welcome to Dolphin Cove Clinic's first percutaneous fixation to the skeleton.'

He began to explain the intricacies of the surgery. He would be implanting an internal peg and plate to each of Moose's rear legs onto which the robotic prosthetics would be attached in three or four weeks' time when the soft tissue had healed.

Everyone leant in as he showed the implant. It was a small but incredibly complex piece of technology. 'If you can see the special coatings here...' he held up the endoprosthesis '...this will become an integral part of Moose's skeleton. In other words, the bone will grow onto the metal of the implant. There are further precautions to ensure a robust, bacteria-proof seal.'

One of the nurses raised her hand. 'Will he be able to walk straight away?'

'Not straight away,' Lucas said, his calm authoritative voice drawing them all in the same way millions of television viewers had been captivated when he'd been the Uber-Vet. Ellie felt a swell of pride she hadn't felt before. Her brainiac nerdy boyfriend from vet school was now an assured, intelligent, passionate veterinarian at the top of his game. It felt incredible to feel pride in place of the darker feelings that had once consumed her— loss and insignificance.

One of the nurses asked about Moose's rehabilitation process.

'Good question,' Lucas said. 'A colleague of mine is coming down from London in a couple of days. A physiotherapist who's worked on a few similar cases with me. She'll work with a couple of local canine physios until they're confident with these specific treatment techniques. By week three, we should have a good idea when he can start using his bionic legs and get on with the business of being a healthy, happy dog.'

'And will Moose stay here at the clinic the entire time?' asked another nurse.

'Yes.' Lucas gave the big old dog's head a loving scrub. 'He'll become a member of the family here for up to four weeks. His own family will be welcome, of course, but I'm sure you'll all join Ellie and me in making him feel at home.'

When their eyes met, Ellie could see a solitary question in them. 'Will you let me stay, too?'

She wanted to. Heaven knew, she did, but…how could she know for sure that Lucas wouldn't change his mind again?

Their eye contact broke.

'Right, everyone! Lucas clapped his hands. 'Let's change a pet's life for the better.'

'Uh-oh.' Maverick looked down at his shirt, where a large blob of strawberry jam had just landed.

Ellie laughed. 'Uh-oh, indeed. I'm guessing you don't want to be wearing strawberry jam on your first day back at school?'

Maverick shook his head. 'Not really. Can I change?'

Normally Ellie would've scrubbed it off,

just as she did all her son's other mishaps, but today was a special day. The first day back at school.

After he'd lifted his arms to have his shirt tugged off,' Maverick threw an anxious look at the door. 'He's coming, right?'

'Absolutely,' Ellie said, hoping her little boy didn't hear the tiniest sliver of concern in her voice.

After the success of Moose's surgery, the three of them had celebrated down at the Hungry Pelican with fish and chips. It had felt like a proper family night out. Grandma and Grandpa had even joined them. The handful of days following the surgery had been a blur. Ensuring Moose had been healing properly, seeing the scores of other pet patients, earmarking the retriever puppies for their increasingly excited puppy handler families and, of course, getting school clothes for Mav.

She glanced at the clock. She'd heard Lucas leave his flat earlier and presumed he'd gone for a run.

Twenty minutes later Ellie gave in to the urge to ring Lucas. They had to leave. Now.

It went straight to voicemail.

Her blood ran cold.

He wasn't doing this. Not on her little boy's big day. She gave Mav's blond curls a stroke. 'Love, I'm just going to run down to the clinic, all right? I'll be back in two.'

Maverick's expectant little face creased with concern. 'Do you think Lucas has had to do a surgery?'

He did that sometimes. Took the out-of-hours calls when she'd had a long day. It had been a welcome reprieve from those first, long months after Drew's surgery when she'd been on call night and day. But usually he consulted her about the case because she knew most of the animals and their histories.

She grabbed her phone to see if there had been any missed calls or texts. 'That's what I'm checking. He could be showing the new physio around.' Or stuck in a ditch. A flat tyre? Or— No. No, he wouldn't have gone to London, would he?

Not today. Surely not today. And not without telling her. His life was here now. At least he'd said he wanted it to be.

She ran down the stairs to the clinic and rounded the corner, only to run into a thirty-something woman holding a duffel bag in her hands. 'Ellie?'

'Hi! Hi…um…' She looked over the woman's shoulder. No Lucas. Crumbs. 'You must be Rebecca, right?'

The specialist physiotherapist gave a nod, her thick specs falling to the tip of her nose.

Ellie looked round again, listening intently for a car. Still no Lucas.

Weird. This wasn't like him.

Rebecca pushed her glasses up and shifted her bag to the other hand. 'Oof! Sorry. My arms are about to fall out of my sockets.' Rebecca shifted her bag again.

Distractedly, Ellie threw her an apologetic smile. 'Would you like to put your bag upstairs?'

'That'd be great. Taking the overnight train down here wasn't the best of decisions. I don't know what made me think I could sleep sitting up!' She yawned and stretched. 'I know it's not the best of intros to make, but I'd like a short kip if I can, before I see Moose.'

'Of course.' Ellie scanned the area again, her eyes darting from building to building see if she could see any lights being turned on.

Nope. Nothing.

Why wasn't she asking Rebecca about Lucas? Surely there was a simple explanation. Like…he'd picked her up at the station and got caught up doing something in the village.

'Did Lucas drive you in?'

'No, he booked a cab for me. Said he had something to do.'

He had to take his son to his first day back at school was what he had to do.

Had she dithered too long about accepting his offer to be a partner? She should've accepted there and then. Whether or not she wanted to marry Lucas shouldn't have been a factor. She was an adult woman who needed to make adult decisions about her son, and her son wanted his father.

She scanned the car park again.

Nope. Nothing.

She was scared. Scared her instincts were right. That Lucas had done a runner.

'Ellie?' Rebecca shifted her bag again.

Ellie's voice sounded foreign to her as she spoke. 'The clinic's not officially open until nine, but the morning nurses are in with him now, so if you like I can let them know you'll be in around ten or eleven?' And then figure out a way to console her son.

'Sounds great,' Rebecca said through another yawn.

Ellie led her up the stairs to the guest flat, where Lucas had made up the sofa bed.

Mav appeared on the balcony outside the two flats, his eyes wide with hope. 'Did you find him?'

This, she thought grimly. *This was why you didn't say yes when he asked to be a partner.*

'No, love. I...' She turned to Rebecca, humiliation sending streaks of heat up into her cheeks. Rebecca's eyes flicked between Ellie and her son. 'Lucas didn't tell you when he'd meet you, did he?'

'Yeah.' She nodded, stifling another yawn. 'He said he'd meet me in the clinic after he did whatever it was he had to do in the morning.'

Right.

Well, at least she knew which way she was leaning on the partner question.

Not a chance, pal.

Not when you hurt her son.

And just then his car pulled into the car park, Lucas bounding out of the driver's seat as soon as the car had lurched to a halt. He looked anxious but happy, his eyes instantly going up to the balcony. When he saw Mav he threw him a big wave. 'Ready for the big day, son?'

'Daddy!' screamed Lucas, barrelling down the stairs to throw himself into Lucas's arms, only to miscalculate the steps and take a terrific tumble.

Lucas could see the accident happening in slow motion. He threw himself towards the stairs but not in time to break Maverick's fall.

No!

He raced to his son, a crumpled heap at the bottom of the stairs, barely looking up when Ellie arrived.

'Don't touch him,' Ellie snapped.

'I just want to—'

'I know.' She held her hand up between them. 'You've done enough.'

It took all his willpower to pull back, but he knew she was right. They needed to call emergency services. Get the first-aid kit. Two people fussing over a boy who might have sustained neck injuries was one person too many.

Ellie pressed her fingers to the side of Mav's throat.

'Pulse?' Lucas whispered.

She nodded. 'Thready, but…' She looked up at him, tears in her eyes. 'Why didn't you tell him to slow down?'

He would've. He'd barely waved before Mav had come running and by then it had been too late. Instead of answering, he pulled out his phone and rang for an ambulance.

Rebecca appeared at the bottom of the steps. 'Anything I can do?' she asked in a low voice. Lucas stood up and took her a few steps from where Ellie was gingerly examining a frightening gash on Maverick's forehead. 'Do you mind going into the clinic? If you go to the back door, one of the nurses will get you the first-aid kit. Wait. No. It'll be faster if I do it. Can you go to the end of the lane?' He tossed her his car keys. 'Flag the ambulance down, okay? This place can be tricky to find.'

He raced into the clinic, grabbed everything he could. A first-aid kit, braces, gauze, antiseptic wipes, instant ice packs. With any luck it would just have been a bad tumble and cut that required a butterfly stitch or two.

By the time he got back, Maverick was lying on his back, his eyes fluttering open, tears pouring down into his ears. 'It hurts, Mummy.'

He tried to pull his right arm to him then began to cry in earnest.

'I know, love. You may have broken it, so—' She cut herself off when she saw Lucas. She gestured for him to hand her the first-aid kit. 'Can you clean up the cut on his forehead? I think it's superficial, but it's just on his hairline. I need to pack his arm in ice until the paramedics get here.'

'I'm sorry, Daddy.'

'What? What are you sorry for?'

'Ruining our first big day together.'

'You didn't ruin a single thing, son. It was just an accident.'

An accident he could see Ellie blamed him for. In a few hours she would've calmed down. He huffed out a breath. In a few hours he had been hoping Ellie would be agreeing to be his wife. That plan would have to go on ice. He spread out all the equipment he'd grabbed from the supplies room.

'Here. Just in case.' He handed Ellie an inflatable neck brace that was meant for canines, but…needs must and all that.

She glanced across at him as he handed her the equipment. 'Thank you.'

There was little warmth in it, but he'd take it. She wasn't telling him to bugger off. Not yet, anyway.

As she saw to Maverick's arm and examined a pair of scraped knees and a bump at the corner of his eye, she issued an odd request. Gauze. Antiseptic wipe. Scissors. She spoke in the same way she would if it were an emergency operation in her clinic, but her voice was utterly bereft of emotion. As if allowing herself to feel anything would pull the seam on whatever it was that was holding her together. A mother's love, no doubt. That, and the core of strength he'd seen in her that very first day they'd met.

He focussed on the cut. The wound, as predicted, was not nearly as bad as it looked. Head wounds always bled a lot and this one was no different. Seeing the streaks of red in his son's hair was unsettling, though. As painful as seeing his father succumb to the cruel effects of Parkinson's. Painful to see and not really be able to do anything. He was cleaning the wound and preparing it for inspection by the paramedics, but really? All he wanted to do was hold Maverick in his arms, pull him in tight and tell him how much he loved him. Apologise again and again, even though he knew it had been an accident. If he just hadn't been so damn excited. Getting the ring had been— It had lit something up in him he had hoped was in there. Strength. Determination. A willingness to be vulnerable. A vulnerability he hadn't expected to have to show so soon.

A car screeched into the car park.

'What the—?' Ellie curled herself protectively over Maverick even though the four-by-four was nowhere near them.

'It's Viola.'

'Why's she here?' Ellie asked, though the answer was pretty obvious. No one drove at high speed into a veterinary clinic before they were open because everything was all right.

Lucas pushed himself up. 'You stay with Mav. I'll go and check.'

Ellie gave him a curt nod. A nod that said, *I wasn't planning on going anywhere, pal.*

He jogged over to Viola's car, reaching her just in time to help her climb out of the enormous vehicle. Her Irish wolfhound, Constanza, was in the passenger seat. Not entirely a health and safety situation to write home about, but it didn't look like Viola was up for a lecture right now.

'Viola? Everything okay?'

She looked more birdlike than ever. And ashen-faced.

'What is it, Viola?'

'It's Wolfgang!'

The mate of Constanza, Wolfgang was Viola's favourite, even though she'd said again and again she knew she shouldn't have one, but she loved Wolfgang to within an inch of her life.

'Where is he?'

'In the back. He's fitting. Last time it was just the once, but this time it won't stop.'

'Last time?' Lucas asked as he ran to the back, trying to get a quick glimpse of Ellie and Mav. She was daubing at his forehead, even though he had been certain he'd stemmed the bleeding.

'Yes.' Viola was following him as he headed to the back of the large four-by-four. 'It was on the day you were doing that fancy surgery and neither you nor Ellie were available and— Oh! I asked them to get Ellie, but they wouldn't!' A huge sob erupted from her small throat. 'I *knew* he wasn't getting the best treatment. Where's Ellie? Can Ellie come out?'

He didn't have to look to know the answer. 'No. There's been an accident.'

'With Ellie?' Viola's legs wobbled.

'No.' He reached out to steady her. 'With Maverick, but…he'll be all right.' He prayed with every fibre in his being that he was right. 'Are you happy for me to treat Wolfgang?'

'You'll do,' Viola said dismissively, her attention no longer on Lucas now that they'd open the back door of the vehicle. 'I just want my boy not to be in any pain.'

Lucas knew that feeling. In spades. It felt physically painful being away from Maverick right now, but one look at Wolfgang and Lucas flew into action. From everything Viola had described about the recurring episodes, Wolfgang was in status epilepticus, a series of epileptic seizures the poor dog had no recovery time between.

He ran back to Ellie and grabbed a roll of gauze for a temporary muzzle.

'What's going on?'

He quickly explained the situation.

Ellie gasped and handed him a pair of scissors and a couple of extra rolls of gauze. 'For his legs if he's really fitting.'

'Would you like to treat him? You know him best.'

'Are you mad? Of course not! My son's lying here bleeding and in pain because of you! Just go! Do your best because Viola's an incredibly important patient. You can do that, can't you? See to a patient without causing even more damage?'

If she'd slapped him it would've hurt less. She blamed him for Maverick's fall. What was worse, she didn't want him anywhere near Maverick.

He quietly turned to go. 'Don't forget to take blood samples after you get the IV in,' she instructed.

'I know.' For her benefit he ran through the list. Blood glucose, electrolytes, packed cell volume. She was stressed. Emotions were getting the better of her. People lashed out when they were scared, and she was definitely scared. He was too but this wasn't the time to show it. He changed his voice, his hand lightly touching Maverick's hair. 'I'm sorry, Ells. I want to be there with you. At the hospital.'

She nodded her acknowledgement but said nothing.

He gave his son's cheek a soft brush with the backs of his fingers then ran back to Viola.

They needed to get the dog on an anti-epileptic drip and onto some oxygen fast. He quickly wrapped the gauze round Wolfgang's muzzle, calling to one of the nurses who'd just come out to check on Maverick to get a gurney. Wolfgang weighed nearly sixty kilos. Lucas was strong. But carrying sixty kilos of fitting wolfhound would not be a wise decision.

He heard sirens approaching as he finished the wrap and tried to get a blanket under the dog so he and the nurse could do a quick transfer.

He glanced over at Ellie. Her ear was cocked. Good. She knew help was on the way. Help she'd accept, anyway.

The veterinary nurse arrived with a gurney just as the ambulance pulled into the drive.

He felt completely torn in two. One of those rock and hard place moments.

Just like he'd found himself in six years ago.

Ellie's business meant the world to her. She'd never let an animal suffer if it was in her means to care for and protect it. He had to be the one to care for and protect her business while she looked after their son. It caused him actual physical pain to not be there by her side, but he wasn't going to screw this up again.

While he slid the dog onto the gurney, he watched helplessly as the paramedic team slid his son onto one and strapped him in.

As they drove away and he ran into the clinic, he prayed he'd made the right decision. That Ellie would realise everything he'd done, he'd done for her.

'Here you are, love.' Ellie's mum handed her a cup of tea. 'I put some sugar in it. For the shock.'

Ellie blew on the cup. 'Thanks, Mum.' She leant against her mother when she sat down in the hard plastic chair beside her.

'Any word from the A and E staff?'

Ellie shook her head. 'Nothing different from what the paramedics said. Double fracture of his arm. They'll put it on soft bandages tonight, a proper cast in a couple of days.'

They both looked at the empty bed where

Maverick had just been. Ellie's voice grew shakier. 'The doctors wanted to do another head scan to make sure there wasn't any damage to his skull. You know, danger of internal bleeding or anything. That's where he is now.'

'And Lucas? Have you heard from him?'

About ninety-seven times. Texts. Calls. To her phone and to the A and E.

Despite herself, she laughed.

Her mother gave her a light nudge. 'Is that a yes or a no?'

'It's a yes.' She flicked a bit of dirt off her knee. 'He's on his way here, actually.'

'Good. I knew you could rely on him.'

'What? Rely on *Lucas*?' Ellie sat up, her tea sloshing over the side of her flimsy plastic cup. 'Ow! God. *Mum!* Do you really think this is the time to wave the Lucas Williams fan club flag?'

Wyn looked at her appraisingly. 'Why? You said it was an accident.'

'It was, but—'

'But what?'

Ellie told her the story. Maverick being so excited. Lucas promising to be there. Lucas not being there. Lucas showing up just when she'd convinced herself he wasn't going to be. Maverick flying down the stairs with no one there to catch him. 'Lucas wasn't there in time. Plain and simple. He never will be. I need to own that now.'

'I thought you said he wasn't here because he was treating Viola's beloved hound?'

'No, Mum!' Ellie whirled on her mother, spilling yet more tea. 'Lucas should've been there for Maverick. Earlier. *Much* earlier than he was. If he'd been there when he'd said he would, Maverick wouldn't have had to run down those bloody stairs and he'd be at school, learning something, and I'd—' She stopped herself. She'd what? Be in Lucas's arms? Be dithering even more about whether or not to say she'd absolutely love him to be a partner in the clinic? Getting on with a thousand other things she'd love to spend the rest of her life doing with Maverick and Lucas by her side.

'It's tough, isn't it?' Wyn said, taking the tea gently from Ellie's hand and placing it on the floor. She handed her a packet of tissues.

'What is?'

'Being so very much in love.'

'Pah! Love? This isn't love. This is pure, unbridled fury. That's what it is.'

'No, it isn't, Eleanor. You know that and you need to stop putting anger in the place of forgiveness. You should've asked that man's forgiveness long ago. Then *none* of you would be in this position.'

'You think I should've asked him to forgive me? For leaving me in the lurch? For swanning off to "help his family"?'

'Eleanor Stone, I did not raise you to be this way. I've tried and tried and tried to get you to see sense through the years but now I'm going to have to be blunt. You were wrong to keep Maverick a secret from him. No matter how angry you were or hurt or heartbroken, you needed to remember that Lucas was in love with you, too. Can you even imagine how painful that must've been? Choosing between you and caring for a family who needed so much help? For a young man like that? It must've been terrifying.'

Ellie pushed her hands between her knees and pressed them tight. It was a good point. One she hadn't fully considered. Definitely not at the time, anyway.

Her mother continued, 'You gave birth to Lucas's son. Anyone who breaks his own heart to look after his own family in their time of need deserves your sympathy. He should be furious with you. If you'd been in his shoes, what would you have done? Sued for custody? I bet you would have.' Her mother was on a roll now. 'So what if he ended up on television? So what if you saw him with some girl on his arm. You didn't wait for facts, did you?'

Ellie bit down on her cheek. No. She hadn't, but he'd broken her heart too and— And what? She'd not considered the fact that he might've had to rip his own heart out to do what he'd done.

She looked at her phone again. Ninety-seven missed calls and messages.

Well.

Ignored calls and messages.

The only reason she knew he was coming was because he'd rung the hospital and got a nurse to tell her he was on his way if she needed to take a break or wanted anything.

Lucas still loved her.

She still loved him.

The only thing that stood between them was fear of something bad happening again, and bad things happened. It didn't mean it would break them up again.

A tear trickled down her cheek. 'I've been a selfish cow, haven't I?'

Her mother wrapped an arm around her and pulled her in for a tight half-hug. 'No, love. You've been a mama bear. Same as I probably would've been.'

'But…' She blinked away her tears. 'I thought you said—'

Her mother cut in. 'Oh, now that I'm old and wise I can see all the mistakes I made and the mistakes you made, too. So you have that to look forward to one day. Being as wise as your old mum.'

'Oh, Mum. I was just so scared.'

'I know, love. Loving a child is terrifying. Trusting someone else to love them as much as you do is just as frightening. Loving a man is terrifying. You don't think I wasn't scared out of my wits when your father suggested we run the pub? Work with the same man day in day out for the rest of my entire life? Trust him to stand by me when I kept putting the wrong ingredients in everyone's orders?' She laughed. 'I remember sending out a Cornish breakfast with Yorkshire puddings once! Imagine. Yorkshire puddings in a Cornish pub.'

Ellie gave her a strange look. 'When did you do that?'

'When I was pregnant with you.'

A twist of guilt tightened in her chest. She'd had some strange quirks when she'd been pregnant. Drew and her parents knew about them, but there had been others she'd silently told Lucas. Quirks only he would've laughed at or sympathised with. The truth was she'd missed him all along. Had picked up the phone she didn't know how many times to ring him when she'd found out she was pregnant, but it had felt so weak!

'The point being, my darling girl...' her mother planted a kiss on top of her head '...loving someone involves a lot of blind trust. Whether you like it or not.'

'I guess that's my problem.' Ellie hiccough-sobbed as she pressed a fresh wad of tissues to her eyes. 'Of course I love Lucas. I guess in order to preserve what little pride I had after he left, I'd convinced myself that he wasn't the kind, amazing, incredible man I'd met, and that if I told him what had happened, he wouldn't love Mav as much as I did. Or me.'

'Not possible,' said a rich voice that definitely wasn't her mother's. 'I love him every bit as much as I love you.'

CHAPTER TEN

Wyn gave Lucas a warm smile, and his arm a pat as she rose from her chair. 'I think that's my cue to go and get some fresh cups of tea.'

When she'd left, Lucas sat down next to Ellie, his heart hammering against his ribcage. 'Is he okay?'

Ellie nodded. 'Broken arm and a few scrapes and bumps. They're doing a final head scan, but it's more precautionary than anything. They think his arm took the brunt of the fall.'

'Ells, I am so sorry. If I hadn't gone out—'

'No. No. It was me. I—I thought you'd gone again. That you'd left us.'

'What?' He cursed his decision not to leave a note. Getting stuck behind a tractor on a narrow country lane definitely hadn't been part of the plan. Neither had dropping by her parents' pub for a 'casual little chat,' but life didn't run by a script, did it?

Ellie threw up her hands and sighed. 'I added two and two and got zero. That's why I was so angry. Not because you were late. Well...' a few more tears welled up in her eyes. 'It was also because you were late, but mostly it was me thinking the worst when you were probably out doing something completely boring, like getting milk for the physio.'

He pressed his hand to his jacket pocket. He had been on an errand. But he'd picked up something much longer lasting than a carton of milk.

'How's Wolfgang?' she sniffled.

'All right. I was a bit worried he'd suffered some brain damage.'

'Why?'

'It took Viola a while to get him into the car.'

Ellie's eyes popped wide open. '*Viola* got him into the car?'

Lucas nodded, every bit as astonished. 'She said she knew she had to get him to the clinic as soon as possible and that it would take too long to wait for us, so...' He laughed. 'She called it Herculean love.'

'What?'

'Whatever it was that enabled her to hoist

that dog into her vehicle. They must weigh about the same.'

Ellie begged to differ. 'Wolfgang weighs more.'

'How do you know?'

'I was worried about her a few months back, so I had her get on the scales with him.'

Lucas grinned. 'But you already knew what he weighed, right?'

'Right.'

'And you've been doing it ever since?'

The bashful smile told him all he needed to know. 'You're amazing, Ells.'

'Why? For secretly weighing my clients?'

'For looking after the pets and their owners so well. No wonder she thinks the world of you.'

Ellie's cheeks pinked up. 'She probably loves you more now that you've saved Wolfgang.'

'No,' Lucas admitted. 'She made it pretty clear the entire time I was treating him that she trusted you far more than she trusted me.'

'Why doesn't she trust you?'

'She said…and I quote… I was "too pretty to trust."'

Ellie hooted with laughter, giggles taking over where the tears had just abated.

Damn, she was beautiful. Oh, hell. He

pulled her into his arms, relief pouring through him when she leant into him and let him take some of the weight. This was as it should've been all those years ago when he'd wanted nothing more than to pull her into his arms when he'd been told his family needed him and he'd had to step away. What an idiot. They'd always been better together. As a team. The fact he'd managed to help his family as well as he had done had been little short of a miracle. One he would've rather shared with Ellie. Nothing had felt entirely right without her. A joke hadn't been as funny. An incredible surgery not as satisfying. The pillow next to his had never been right—not without that fan of flame-gold hair spread across it. It was an emptiness he'd felt as acutely as if he'd lost a limb. And yet he'd thought he'd done the right thing, stoically 'setting her free'. All those years gaslit by his own stupid decision-making.

Hindsight. Hindsight could be a real bitch.

'I was wrong, Ells. To do what I did.'

'What? On the stairs?'

'No, not that.' He checked himself when she stiffened. 'Obviously, that. Of course I wish I'd caught him. The last thing I want is for Maverick to suffer even the slightest pain. He fell so far down the stairs. I just couldn't get there in time. Believe me, Ellie. If it had been within my power, I would've been there.'

Just as he knew in his heart he would've been there for her if he'd known about Maverick all along.

'I know,' she said, crying again. After a few jagged breaths, she pushed herself back from his chest and looked him in the eye. 'I know it was an accident and I owe you an apology for reacting so poorly.'

'No. Ells—'

She cut him off. 'See this?' She pointed to a small chip on one of her teeth.

'Yes.'

'I got that when I was rollerblading towards my mum and she turned around to say something to my father just as I fell flat on my face.'

'Ouch.' He grimaced. 'Remember this?' He pulled up his sleeve and pointed to a scar on the inside of his arm.

She stared at it a moment then smiled sheepishly. '*Crumbs*. Was that the time Drew was supposed to be holding the barbed wire up for you when we were trying to get through a fence to an injured deer?'

'Sure was.'

Ellie clapped her hand to her mouth. 'And

I was the one who distracted Drew, who let go of the barbed wire and...'

'Rip!' Lucas said, smiling at the memory. They'd all stared at his wound in horror, then Ellie had done some lightning-fast triage on him whilst barking orders at Drew to help the deer that had got itself properly stuck in someone's chain-link fence. They'd all gone out for drinks together afterwards and laughed and laughed. Not a cross word between them. There never had been. Any problems? They'd talked them out.

'Didn't I buy a nurse's uniform to wear when I changed your wound dressing?' Ellie tipped her head to the side, a tumble of curls shifting onto her forehead.

'Yes, you did.' He nodded, teasing her hair away with a finger. 'I seem to remember you wearing it more than once.'

'That nurse's uniform saw quite a bit of action over the years, didn't it?'

'Yes, it did,' Lucas confirmed with a grin, and then, more seriously, said, 'But not just because we were hurt.'

'No.' Ellie's smile faltered. 'No, it was for other things, too.'

Lucas took one of her hands in his. 'Ells, I know things are crazy complicated between us, but... I love you. And I know it's only been a few weeks, but I love Mav, too. Fell in love with him every bit as fast as I fell in love with you. I know this is hilarious coming from me, but…'

'But what?'

He looked her straight in the eye. 'Don't you think we'd be better off doing this together? As a team? A proper team?'

Ellie felt a lump form in her throat. She was pretty sure Lucas wasn't talking about being a business partner this time.

He dug into his pocket and produced a small red box. 'I know the timing isn't perfect and the setting is about as opposite to romantic as you can get, but… Ellie Stone? Would you do me the honour of being my wife?'

'In sickness and in health?' she asked, even though she knew she didn't need to.

'Better. Worse. Richer. Poorer. Stressed. Chillaxed. But mostly? To love and to cherish.'

She watched as he popped open the box.

It was a new ring. Completely different from the one he'd proposed with all those years ago. It didn't look immaculately smooth like a traditional engagement ring. No shiny solitaire. She'd never liked those really. Had said she'd wanted the perfect veterinarians' ring but wasn't quite sure what that was.

This was it.

'It's sand cast,' Lucas explained. 'I was at the jeweller's this morning, picking it up.'

'Sand cast?'

'Yup. I hadn't heard of it either, but I wanted something Cornish.'

'Why?'

'To prove to you I see my future here, with you and Mav.'

She looked into his eyes and saw nothing but love in them. Genuine commitment. And, most importantly, trust.

She picked up the ring and held it up to the light. Did she share that level of trust? Have the blind faith her mother said she needed to have to pull together as a couple?

'It's an eternity ring,' Lucas said, pointing to the tiny ring of glittering jewels tucked into the delicate white gold band. 'Sapphires for the sea. Diamonds for the stars. And, of course, some sand from Dolphin Cove.'

'It's beautiful.'

'Not as beautiful as you are, Ells.'

She tipped her forehead to his. 'Do you think we can do it this time? Trust one another with our problems? Even when they seem insurmountable?'

He pulled back and tipped her chin up so that their eyes met. '*Especially* when they seem insurmountable. We did pretty well this morning, didn't we? Miscommunications aside.'

'I think next time—if there is one...' Their eyes met as Ellie began to giggle. Together they said, 'There will be more than one.'

Lucas dropped a kiss on her forehead then, pulling back, his gaze dropped to the ring. 'Is that a yes?'

Her heart skipped a beat when she saw just how hopeful he looked.

'It's a yes,' she said, grinning like a loon as he slipped the ring on her finger.

Mid-kiss they heard a throat being cleared.

'Mum!' Ellie's cheeks flamed red, but she didn't care. Not any more. 'Sorry. We... um—'

'I take it you said yes, then?' her mother asked.

Lucas looked at Wyn in surprise. 'How did you know I'd propose here?'

She tapped the side of her head. 'I'm a wise old thing. Never forget that. Especially now that I'm going to be your mother-in-law.'

Lucas gave her a jaunty sailor's salute. 'Yes, ma'am.'

Wyn gave a curtsy then pulled the curtain

open wider. 'I think you both might want to share your news with this young man.'

'Mum!' Maverick ran to his mother, pulling himself short of a hug to protect his arm. When he saw Lucas beside her his smile doubled. 'Daddy! Look! I'm going to have a scar!'

Lucas laughed. 'I have it on good authority women like a man with a scar or two.' He dropped Ellie a wink that unleashed a spray of heat inside her. He was mostly right. It wasn't the scars she loved. It was the man who'd weathered the pain and come out the other side smiling.

She held up her hand and wriggled her ring finger.

Maverick went wide-eyed and gave a dramatic, 'Ooh!' His eyes ping-ponged between the pair of them, absorbing their happy smiles, and then he burst into tears.

Both Ellie and Lucas dropped to their knees and, being careful of his arm, help him, whispered consoling words and, thanks to a handkerchief Lucas produced, wiped away his tears.

'Love, do you not want us to get married?' Ellie asked.

'I do!' Maverick insisted, a smile finally breaking through the wash of tears. 'I really,

really do! This is me being happy!' His watery blue eyes landed on Lucas. 'Does that mean you're going to stay?'

Lucas gently combed his fingers through his son's hair. 'That it does, son. That it does. For ever and a day.'

'Yippee!' Maverick cried, then yelped as he'd stretched out his arm with joy.

After a quick check with the doctor, who confirmed Maverick's scan was fine and that the only further treatment he'd need was for his arm, they were ready to go home. As a family.

Ellie's mum doled out kisses and invited everyone to the pub for supper, but only if they were up to it. They all agreed they would definitely be up to it, particularly when Lucas asked Wyn to make sure there was some chilled champagne ready for their arrival.

After Wyn left, Ellie gave Maverick her hand to hold. 'Shall we get you home, love?'

'Yes, please.' He nodded then threw a hopeful look up at Lucas. 'By for ever, you mean you'll be coming to the Christmas play?'

'I'll be coming to all of the Christmas plays, Mav,' Lucas confirmed. 'Wild horses wouldn't keep me away.'

'Good! Because Mummy says the wild

horses have to stay out on the moor and that they're actually tame.'

Ellie shot Lucas an embarrassed look. No more pulling the wool over his eyes on that front.

'And this year?' Maverick sent Ellie a mischievous look. 'I've decided what I really want to be in the nativity is Barnacle!'

The laugh the three of them shared meant so much more to Ellie than she could have ever explained. It was a laugh built on happiness, hope and the loving expectation of many more times like this to come. A love that would grow and enrich all their lives. A love she couldn't wait to share.

CHAPTER ELEVEN

'THIS IS BONKERS, RIGHT?' Ellie grinned at
Drew as he put the flower crown on her head.

'Yes, but I wouldn't expect anything less
from you. Where's my right-hand man?'

'Mav? He's trying to put all the puppies
onto leads without them getting tangled up,
all with just one arm'

'Ha! That'll be interesting. And Esmerelda?'

'She's with Lucas.'

They both glanced out of the window of her
flat towards the beach cove, but Drew pulled
the curtain across before Ellie could see the
full scene. The sudden movement made him
wobble.

Ellie reached out to steady him. 'Are you
sure you're up for the walk down the aisle?'

Drew brandished his 'fancy' cane. 'I'll be
fine. Are you sure your father doesn't mind
I'm going to be sharing the walk with him?'

'What?' Ellie feigned disbelief. 'The man

who single-handedly dragged his little girl out of her funk by helping her create one of the best vet clinics this side of London? He's honoured.' Her smile softened. 'He really is, Drew. Besides...' her grin returned to full wattage '...he thinks eloping on the beach next to Dolphin Cove is akin to eloping in Timbuktu, so...you're helping him in foreign climes.'

A car horn tooted. 'Speaking of foreign climes...' Drew nodded towards the car park '...it looks like the Londoners have arrived.'

Ellie ran to the window, grinning as Lucas jogged out to the car park, pulling his brother into a huge bear hug the second he got out of the car. His mum had come as well. Her body language spoke of a shyer disposition, but even from up at the flat Ellie could see the pride in her face.

Ten minutes later Maverick headed down to the cove with all ten Labrador puppies sort of under control. He made his way down the aisle past friends, family and the staff from the clinic, as if he was the King of Cornwall himself. It was hilarious. Her mum was beaming away at the front, as was Lucas's mother. The vicar, who'd brought his cat in the day after Ellie had agreed to marry Lucas, had barely lifted a brow when they'd asked him to marry them just as soon as humanly possible. Love, he said, waited for nothing and no one and, as they were promising a fish pie and pints at the pub after, why not?

Lucas's eyes lifted from his son's to hers. A smile so proud and happy filled his face she couldn't help but return it. Though her father was on one arm and Drew was on the other, she only had eyes for one man. The gorgeous blond she couldn't wait to call her husband.

When it came time to exchange vows, the vicar took a step back, knowing they had written the vows themselves and needed no prompting to say what was already in their hearts.

Lucas took Ellie's hands in his, his eyes shining with happiness. 'Ellie Stone? I promise here in front of everyone we love to be your best friend.' He threw an apologetic smile to their shared best man. 'Sorry, Drew. I know you're up there, but… I think it's a post that has room for more.'

'You're not wrong there, mate.' Drew nodded his approval. 'You've always been welcome.'

'Thank you,' Lucas said, from his heart. He turned back to Ellie, his eyes connecting with hers with such depth of emotion she could feel it in her soul. 'I promise never to keep anything from you. Even if it causes one or both of us pain. I know now that a burden shared is a burden halved and that together we can turn that pain into something that will heal and help us grow even stronger. Unless, of course, it's Christmas or your birthday and then all bets are off.'

The small crowd laughed and filled the air with a few hoots of appreciation.

Lucas kissed her cheek. 'I promise to love you. To honour you. To respect you, but most of all I promise to cherish you and our family as the most important, precious people in my life. With you...you and Mav... I know we can do anything. Achieve anything.'

Ellie said her own vows with matching intensity. How could she not? She finally felt whole again. Whole after learning so much about herself and life and now, most importantly, love.

After they'd exchanged rings, the vicar pronounced them husband and wife. 'I suppose you'd like to kiss the bride?'

'I thought you'd never ask,' said Lucas, already pulling Ellie into his arms. From the moment their lips touched, Ellie knew they'd made exactly the right choice to wed straight away. Love didn't wait. So when you had it? She knew they had courage on their side as they embarked on their new lives together, as a family.

* * * * *

*Look out for the next story in the
Dolphin Cove Vets duet*

Healing the Vet's Heart
by Annie Claydon

*And if you enjoyed this story, check out
these other great reads from Annie O'Neil*

Risking Her Heart on the Single Dad
Making Christmas Special Again
A Return, a Reunion, a Wedding

All available now!